Andy Griffiths has a body with over 68 working parts. When not writing (with his hands), Andy enjoys reading (with his eyes), thinking (with his brain), running (with his legs), swimming (with his arms and legs), breathing (with his nose, trachea, and lungs), eating (with his mouth, teeth, tongue, and saliva), digesting his food (with his small intestine, large intestine, gallbladder, pancreas, liver, and spleen) and sitting (on his butt). That is all there is to know about Andy Griffiths.

Terry Denton also has a body. It is taller, older, and much better-looking than Andy's body. That is all there is to know about Terry Denton.

ALSO BY ANDY GRIFFITHS
AND ILLUSTRATED BY TERRY DENTON
The Cat on the Mat Is Flat
The Big Fat Cow That Goes Kapow
Killer Koalas from Outer Space and Lots of Other
Very Bad Stuff that Will Make Your Brain Explode!

ANDY GRIFFITHS

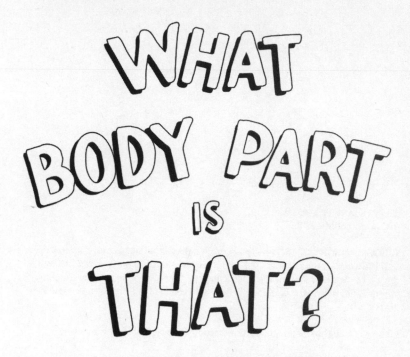

WHAT BODY PART IS THAT?

ILLUSTRATED BY
TERRY DENTON

FEIWEL AND FRIENDS • NEW YORK

A FEIWEL AND FRIENDS BOOK
An Imprint of Macmillan

WHAT BODY PART IS THAT? Text copyright © 2011 by Backyard Stories Pty Ltd. Illustrations copyright © 2011 by Terry Denton. All rights reserved. Printed in the United States of America by R. R. Donnelley & Sons Company, Harrisonburg, Virginia. For information, address Feiwel and Friends, 175 Fifth Avenue, New York, N. Y. 10010.

Library of Congress Cataloging-in-Publication Data Available

ISBN: 978-0-312-36790-9

Book design by Katie Cline

Feiwel and Friends logo designed by Filomena Tuosto

This book was originally published in Australia by Pan Macmillan Australia Pty Limited.

First published in the United States by Feiwel and Friends, an imprint of Macmillan

First U.S. Edition: 2012

10 9 8 7 6 5 4 3 2 1

mackids.com

Contents

Introduction

There is a lot of nonsense written about the human body, and this book is no exception.

In its 68 fully illustrated, 100 percent fact-free chapters, *What Body Part Is That?* will explain everything you ever needed to know about your body without the boring technical jargon and scientific accuracy that normally clog up the pages of books of this type.

Never again will you be stuck for an answer when somebody comes up to you, points at a part of your body and demands to know, "What body part is that?"

That is all there is to know about this book.

YOUR BODY:
A quick reference guide

Don't have time to read the whole book?
Use this quick reference guide to select the body part
you'd like to find out about and go straight there.

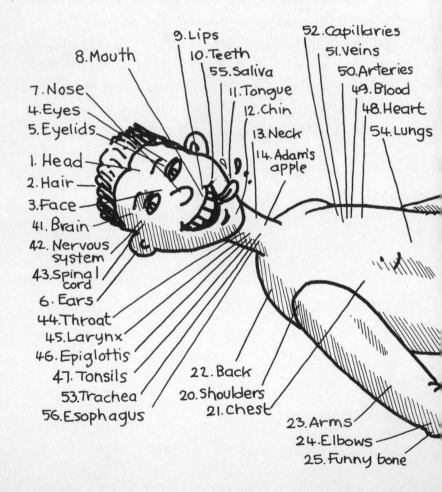

8. Mouth
9. Lips
10. Teeth
55. Saliva
11. Tongue
12. Chin
13. Neck
14. Adam's apple
52. Capillaries
51. Veins
50. Arteries
49. Blood
48. Heart
54. Lungs

7. Nose
4. Eyes
5. Eyelids
1. Head
2. Hair
3. Face
41. Brain
42. Nervous system
43. Spinal cord
6. Ears
44. Throat
45. Larynx
46. Epiglottis
47. Tonsils
53. Trachea
56. Esophagus

22. Back
20. Shoulders
21. Chest
23. Arms
24. Elbows
25. Funny bone

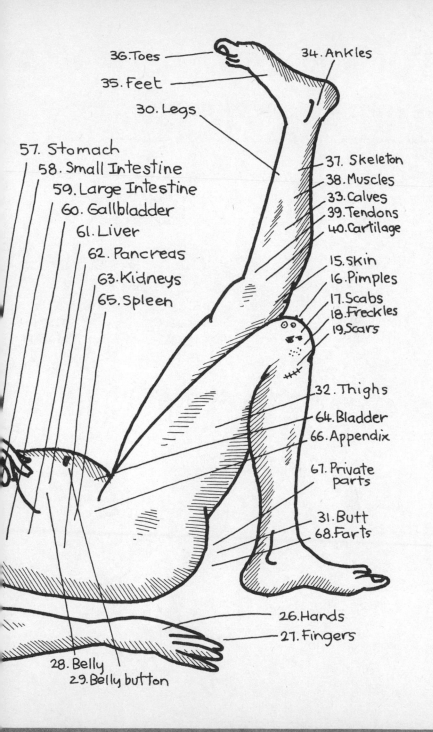

36. Toes

34. Ankles

35. Feet

30. Legs

57. Stomach

58. Small Intestine

59. Large Intestine

60. Gallbladder

61. Liver

62. Pancreas

63. Kidneys

65. Spleen

37. Skeleton

38. Muscles

33. Calves

39. Tendons

40. Cartilage

15. Skin

16. Pimples

17. Scabs

18. Freckles

19. Scars

32. Thighs

64. Bladder

66. Appendix

67. Private parts

31. Butt

68. Farts

26. Hands

27. Fingers

28. Belly

29. Belly button

The Parts You Can See

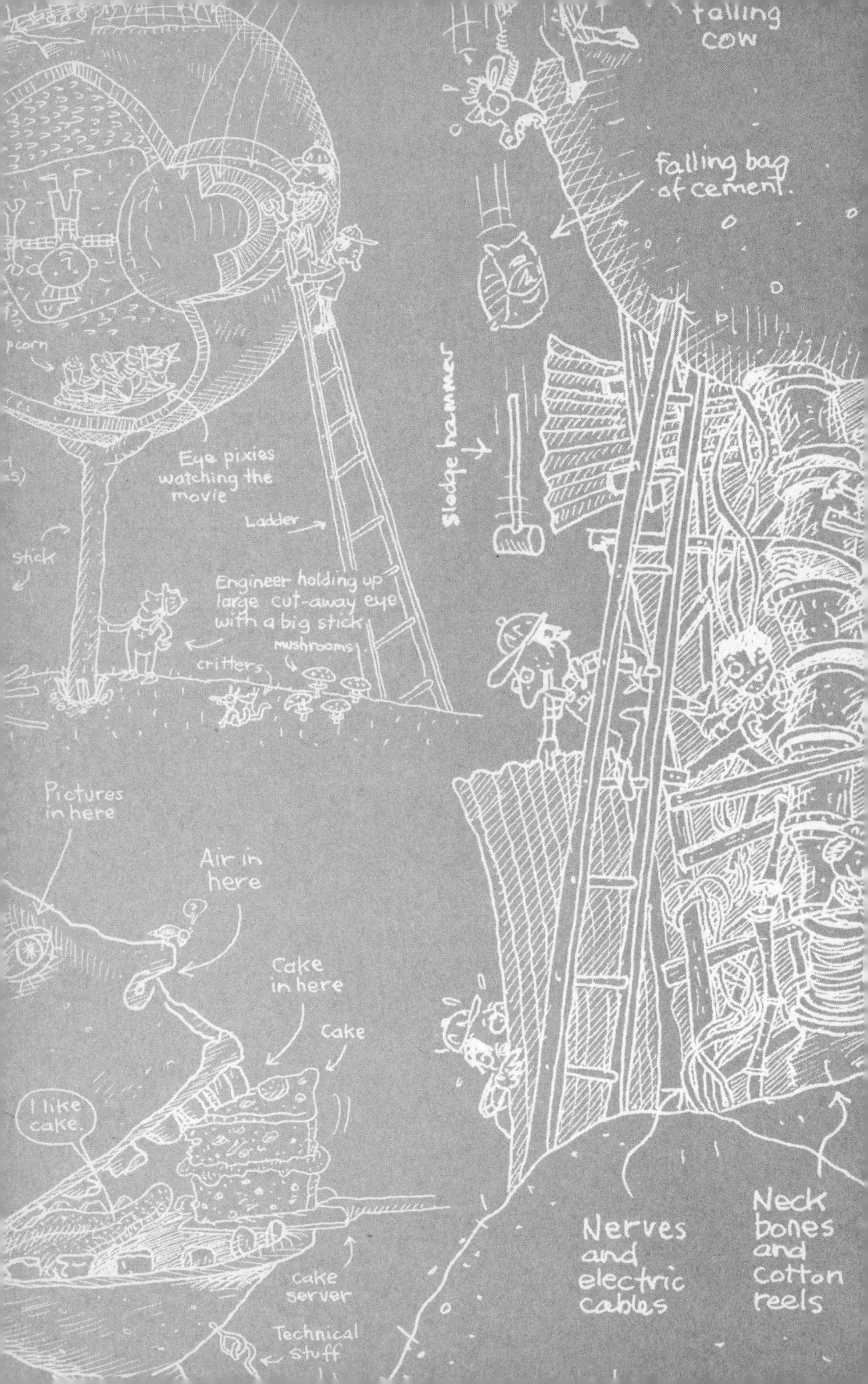
falling cow
Falling bag of cement.
Sledge hammer
Eye pixies watching the movie
Ladder
stick
Engineer holding up large cut-away eye with a big stick
mushrooms
critters
Pictures in here
Air in here
Cake in here
Cake
I like cake.
cake server
Technical stuff
Nerves and electric cables
Neck bones and cotton reels

SECTION 1

Head & Neck

In this section, you will find out everything there is to know about the head and neck.

1. Head

Your head sits on top of your neck.

It has seven holes: two eye holes, two ear holes, two nose holes, and one cake hole.

You put pictures into your eye holes, sounds into your ear holes, air into your nose holes, and cakes into your cake hole. (You can also put a wide variety of healthy fresh fruits and vegetables into your cake hole, but I mostly use mine for cake.)

That is all there is to know about your head.

A&T'S FUN BODY PART FACT #1

In ancient times, there was a race of people who used to carry their heads under their arms.

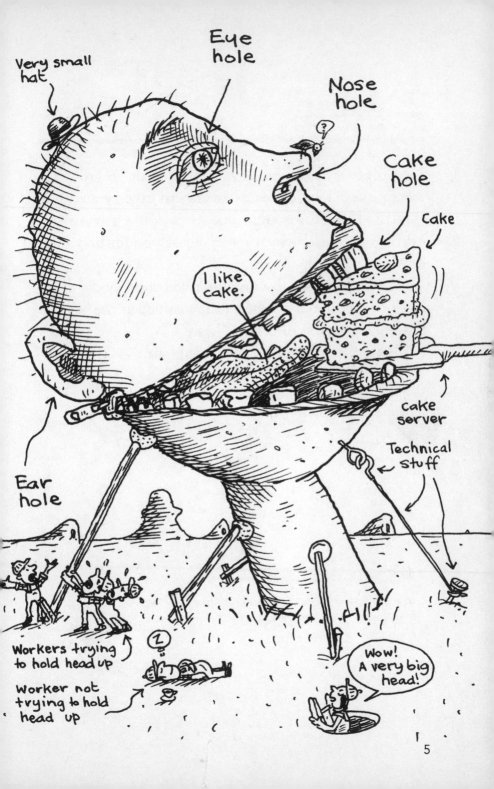

5

2. Hair

Hair is a hairy hair-like growth called "hair." It grows mostly out of a heady head-like growth called your "head," which grows out of a necky neck-like growth called your "neck," which grows out of a bodily body-like growth called your "body."

The bodily body-like growth called your "body" also has lots of hair, but nowhere near as much as the heady head-like growth called your "head."

That is all there is to know about hair.

A&T'S FUN BODY PART FACT #2

In ancient times, people used to grow their hair really long and wrap it around their bodies because clothes hadn't been invented yet.

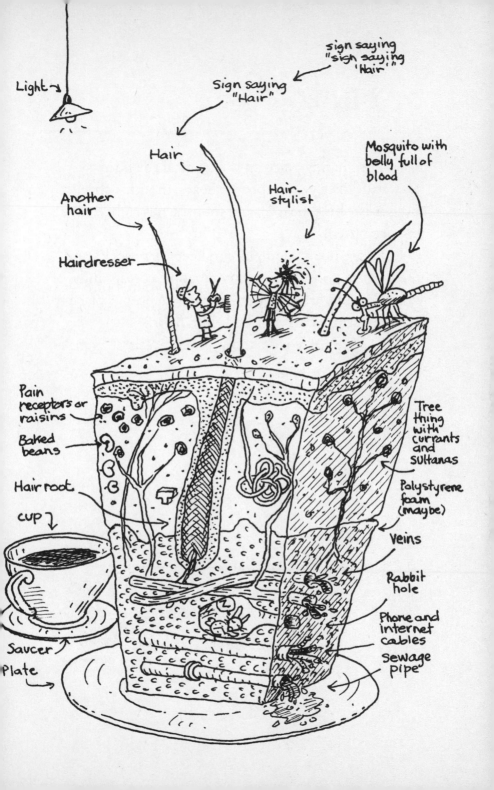

3. Face

Faces are a handy place on the front of the head to keep stuff like eyes, eyebrows, noses, mouths, cheeks, foreheads, chins, beards, and moustaches right where you need them.

Faces are not a good place to keep dirty socks and underpants, sporting equipment, apple cores, candy wrappers, and other bits of trash. (The proper place to keep this stuff is on your bedroom floor.)

That is all there is to know about faces.

A&T'S FUN BODY PART FACT #3

Every year in Australia, more than 300 people have their faces ripped off by killer koalas from outer space.

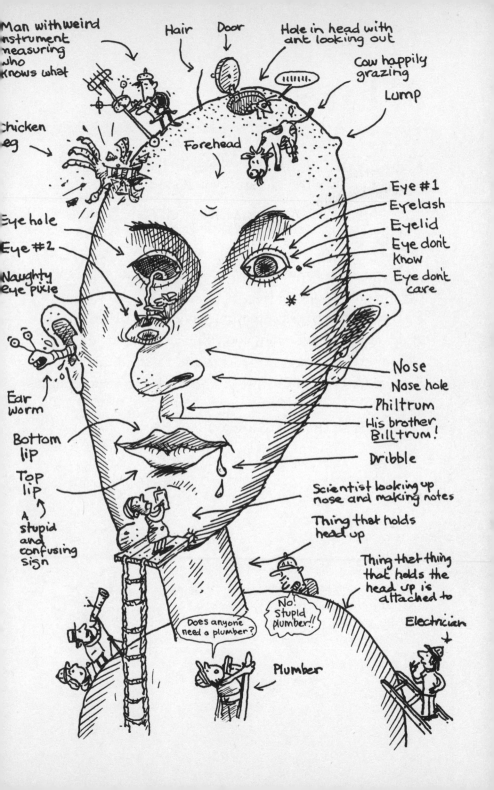

4. Eyes

Your eyes are two soft balls of jelly that help you to see stuff, but only when the stuff you need to see is right in front of you.

If you want to see stuff that is very far away, you will need a telescope.

If you want to see stuff that is really small, you will need a microscope.

If you want to see something that's in a locked room and you don't have a key, you will need to take one of your eyeballs out of its socket and roll it under the door. (Don't forget to rinse your eyeball before you put it back in.)

That is all there is to know about eyes.

A&T'S FUN BODY PART FACT #4

If you're walking around an old abandoned house late at night and you see a pair of eyeballs floating in midair, then you should get out of there immediately because those eyeballs probably belong to a GHOST!

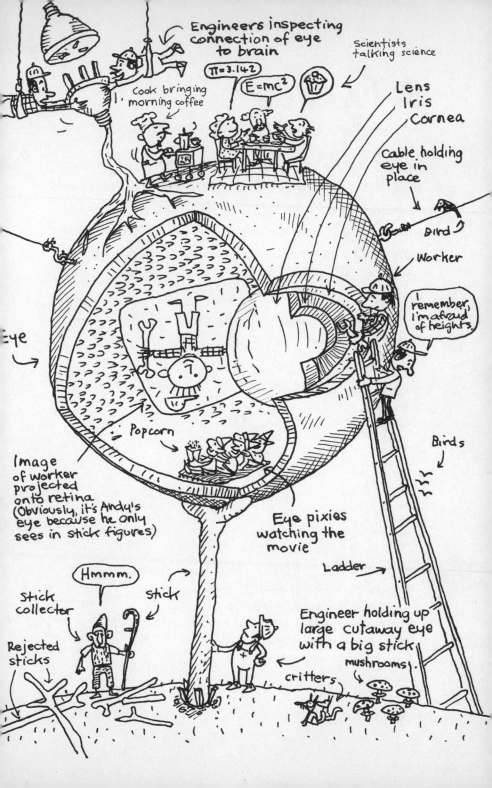

5. Eyelids

Eyelids are conveniently located eyeball-sized flaps of skin that can be drawn down instantly to protect your eyeballs from bright lights, sandstorms, scary movies, sparks, people without clothes on, naked people, naked people without clothes on, people with clothes on but who are really naked underneath, onion fumes, and the sharp end of pointy sticks.

That is all there is to know about eyelids.

A&T'S FUN BODY PART FACT #5

Humans are the only animals that can blink *and* wink. All other animals can blink but they never wink. Unless, of course, they are doing it behind our backs when we're not looking.

EYELIDS
and OTHER KINDS OF LIDS

Turkish head lid →

Eyelids

Top head lid →

English head lid ↗

Drink cup lid ↓

Other head lid ↙

Do you like any of these lids?

Nah!

Salt shaker lid →

Weird lid →

Meat serving lid ↓

Manhole lid ↓

Saucepan lid

Old garbage can lid ↓

Plug hole lid ↙

Bottletop lid ↓

Salad dressing lid →

Whiskey bottle lid ↑

Gopher nose lid

Press the button and stuff comes out lid

Soap dispenser lid

Cheese board lid ↗

Odd-shaped lid for some long-lost kitchen container

Small pot lid ↑

Silver bald man's head lid ↑

6. Ears

Ears can be big or small, depending on their size.

They can be white, pink, brown or black, depending on their color, and they can be round, oval, or pointy, depending on their shape.

Ears can be clean or dirty, depending on how clean or dirty they are, and they can be especially handy for receiving important instructions and advice from your parents and teachers, depending on whether you can be bothered listening to them or not.

That is all there is to know about ears.

A&T'S FUN BODY PART FACT #6

When you go up to a high elevation, your ears pop. If you go up too high, however, your whole head will explode.

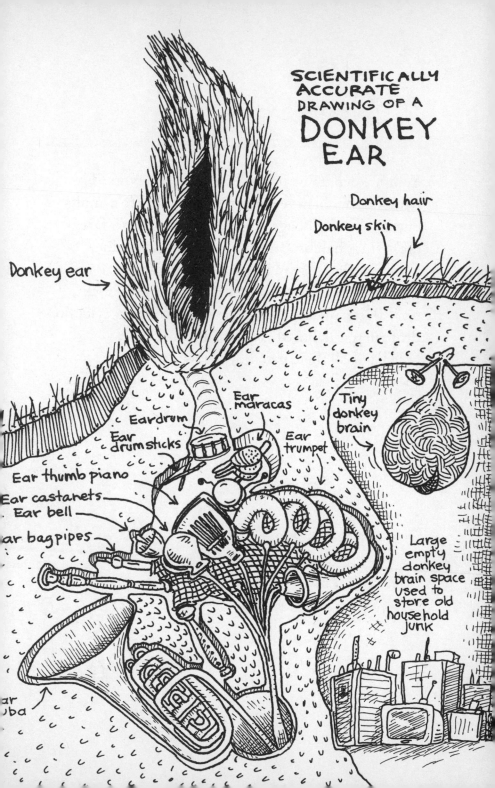

7. Nose

Your nose contains five million odor receptors. This is why you should never put your nose close to armpits, butts, cooked cabbage, dog poo, elbow grease, farts, gross stuff, halitosis, infected sores, jocks, kidney worms, locker rooms, maggots, nasty diapers, onions, poop-throwing monkeys, rotten eggs, smelly socks, toxic waste, underpants, vegetables, wee-wee, xylophone droppings, yak breath, or zoo animals.

That is all there is to know about noses.

A&T'S FUN BODY PART FACT #7

Your thumb is the same length as your nose.

Cool!!

8. Mouth

The mouth is the entry point for fresh air, food, and liquid, and the exit point for used air, words, and burps.

Some talented people are able to burp their words. Some can even burp the whole alphabet. Unfortunately, I am not one of them. I tried once, but I only got as far as the letter "e" before I was sick all over myself. Oh yeah, the mouth is also the exit point for vomit.

That is all there is to know about mouths.

A&T'S FUN BODY PART FACT #8

More than 298 billion million bacteria live in your mouth. Think about that next time you're tempted to kiss someone (*see* LIPS, page 20).

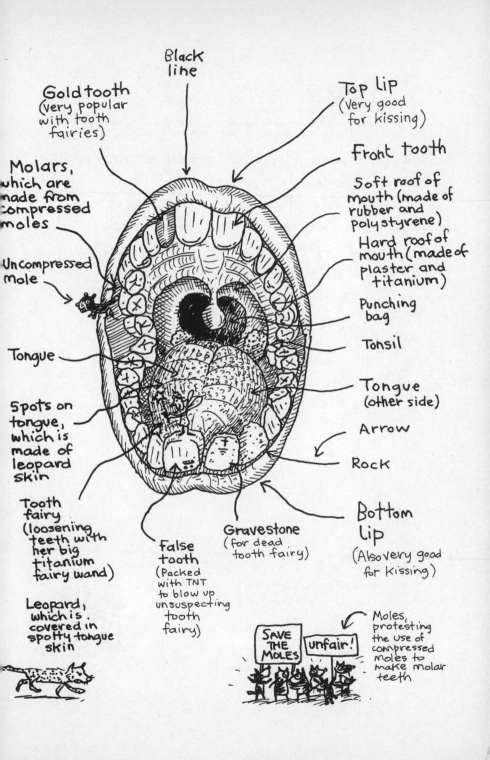

Black line

Gold tooth (very popular with tooth fairies)

Top Lip (Very good for kissing)

Front tooth

Molars, which are made from compressed moles

Soft roof of mouth (made of rubber and polystyrene)

Hard roof of mouth (made of plaster and titanium)

Uncompressed mole

Punching bag

Tonsil

Tongue

Tongue (other side)

Spots on tongue, which is made of leopard skin

Arrow

Rock

Tooth fairy (loosening teeth with her big titanium fairy wand)

Bottom Lip (Also very good for kissing)

False tooth (Packed with TNT to blow up unsuspecting tooth fairy)

Gravestone (for dead tooth fairy)

Leopard, which is covered in spotty tongue skin

SAVE THE MOLES

unfair!

Moles, protesting the use of compressed moles to make molar teeth

9. Lips

Lips are made of 100 percent lip meat and are generally found on the outside of your mouth.

Lips are one of the most important parts of your body because without lips you wouldn't be able to talk properly, use straws, wear lipstick, get lip piercings, or make pretend farting noises.

Some people like to press their lips up against other people's lips. This is called "kissing" and should be avoided at all costs.

If you see kissers approaching, you should run away as fast as you can in case you are next.

That is all there is to know about lips.

A&T'S FUN BODY PART FACT #9

International Kissing Day is July 6th, so on that day remember to stay home and lock the doors.
You have been warned. . . .

If you had to kiss one of the above pairs of lips, which pair would you choose?

10. Teeth

Teeth are small, hard, white things that help you to chew your food and to bite people.

Most people do not like being bitten, so if you are going to bite somebody, you'd better make it fast and run away before they can bite you back.

If somebody bites *you*, clean and disinfect the wound thoroughly, taking care to remove any teeth that may remain in your flesh, and then cry really loudly so that the person who bit you gets into the maximum amount of trouble that it is possible for somebody who has bitten somebody else to get into.

That is all there is to know about teeth.

A&T'S FUN BODY PART FACT #10

A Chinese dentist once built a tower out of 28 million human teeth. Unfortunately, he neglected to include doors or windows, was trapped inside, and never seen again.

Help! Get me out of here.

Teeth

11. Tongue

Your tongue is the part of your body that you use to lick stuff.

Good stuff to lick is ice cream, icy poles, fresh dew, chocolate, lollipops, lickable wallpaper, cake mixture, the car after it's been raining, and anything that's bubble gum flavored.

Bad stuff to lick is dirt, dirty floors, a road, cheese in a mousetrap, moldy cheese in a mousetrap, a door handle, a bathroom door handle, a toilet seat, a dog's face, a dog's tongue, your finger after you've put it in your ear, and a used Band-Aid.

That is all there is to know about tongues.

A&T'S FUN BODY PART FACT #11

There are 9,000 taste buds on the tongue. Of these 9,000 taste buds, 8,999 think that brussels sprout are disgusting. The other one is wrong.

Yuk!!!

Brussels sprout

Tongue

Mum!

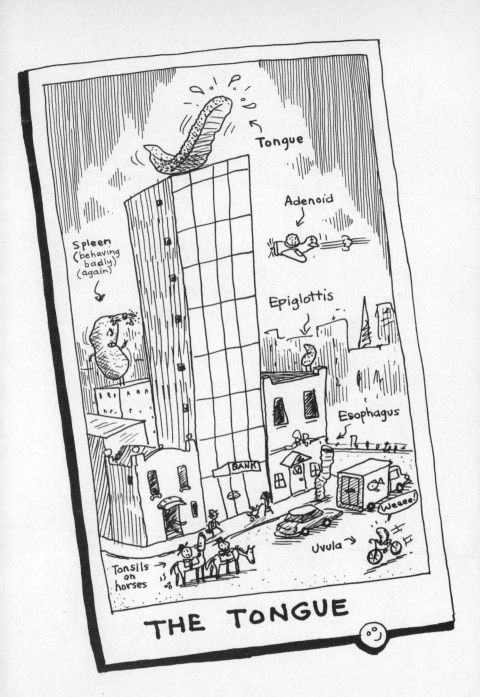

THE TONGUE

12. Chin

Your chin is located directly beneath your mouth.

If you want to make yourself look smarter than you actually are, try gently stroking your chin with your thumb and forefinger.

Do not stroke your chin too quickly or it will simply look like your chin is itchy.

It is also important to use the finger and thumb of the same hand, otherwise you will just end up looking like an idiot.

If you do this correctly, everyone will be convinced you are very smart and thinking deep thoughts, when all you're really thinking about is what you are going to have for lunch.

That is all there is to know about chins.

A&T'S FUN BODY PART FACT #12

If a big, bad wolf is knocking on your door and saying, "Let me in!" a clever thing to say is, "Not by the hair of my chinny-chin-chin!"

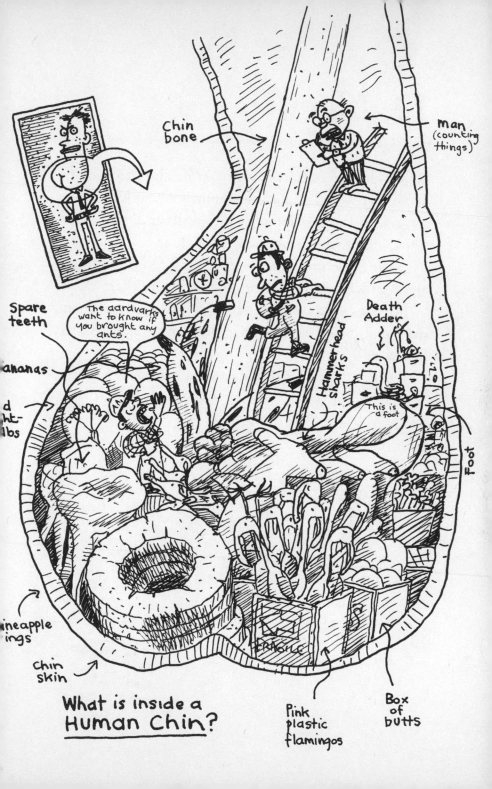

13. Neck

If we didn't have necks to hold our heads onto our bodies, we would all just be a bunch of headless bodies staggering around, bumping into walls and falling down stairs, and we'd never get anything done.

Meanwhile, our heads would just be rolling around all over the place, not getting much done either.

So, our necks are pretty important—without them, we'd all just be a bunch of headless freaks and freaky heads.

That is all there is to know about necks.

A&T'S FUN BODY PART FACT #13

Q: Why do giraffes have such long necks?
A: Because they have really smelly feet.

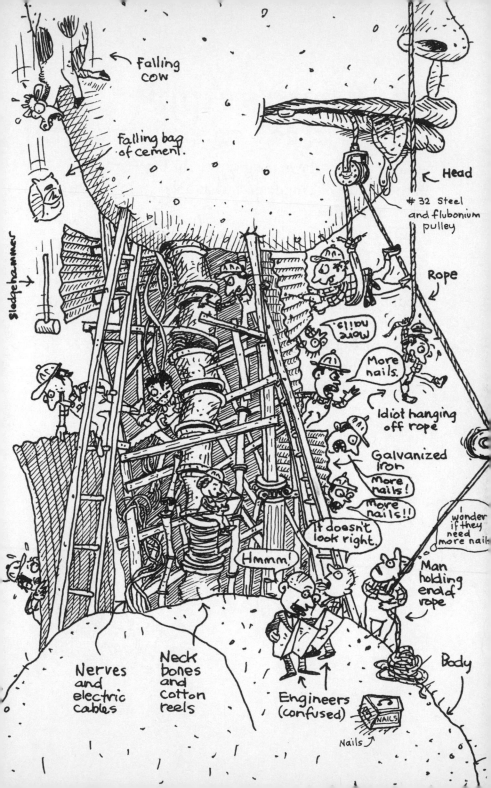

14. Adam's Apple

Adam's apple is the name given to the big weird lump in the middle of a man's neck that bobs up and down when he swallows.

Other names for this big weird lump are: Bob's banana, Carl's kumquat, Fred's fig, Greg's grape, Malcolm's mango, Leon's lemon, Peter's passion fruit, Rodney's raspberry, Terry's tomato, and Walter's watermelon.

No matter what you call it, though, it's still just a big weird lump in the middle of a man's neck.

That is all there is to know about Adam's apples.

A&T'S FUN BODY PART FACT #14

Cosmetic surgery to reduce the size of the Adam's apple is called chondrolaryngoplasty.

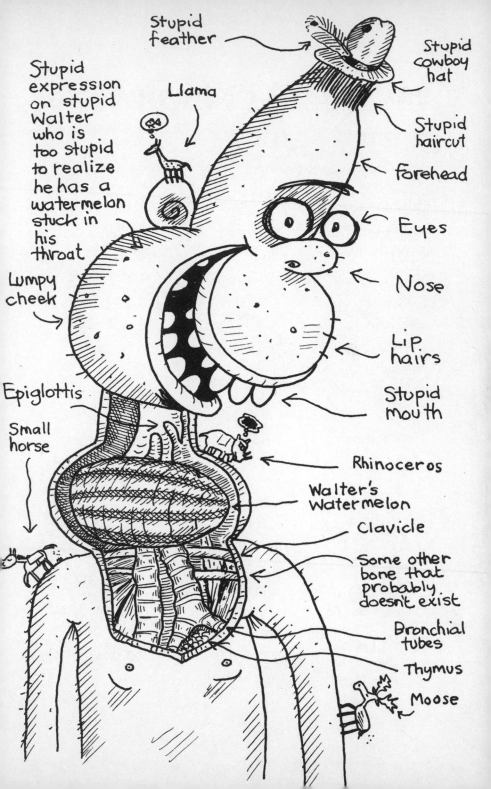

FACIAL EXPRESSIONS:
A handy guide

Human faces are capable of 123 different expressions. Here's a handy guide to help you to identify and correctly interpret some of the most important ones.

Happy

Bored

What's that?

Yikes! Something's falling!

It's a fridge about to crash onto my head!!

AARRGHHHH!!

SECTION 2

Skin

Skin! It's here! It's there! It's all over your body!
But what exactly is skin and how does it work?
Here is everything there is to know about skin.

15. Skin

Imagine having a really cool suit that fit you perfectly no matter what size you were!

And imagine if it helped to warm you up when you're cold and cool you down when you're hot.

And imagine if it protected you from germs, repaired itself if it was torn or ripped and, best of all, it stopped your guts falling out onto the ground and being eaten by wild dogs!

Well, the great news is that you already have a suit exactly like this. It's called your "skin" and you get one free when you're born.

That is all there is to know about skin.

A&T'S FUN BODY PART FACT #15

The skin is the body's largest organ. It is about 2 millimeters thick, weighs 7 pounds, and comes in a wide range of fashionable and stylish colors to suit any nationality.

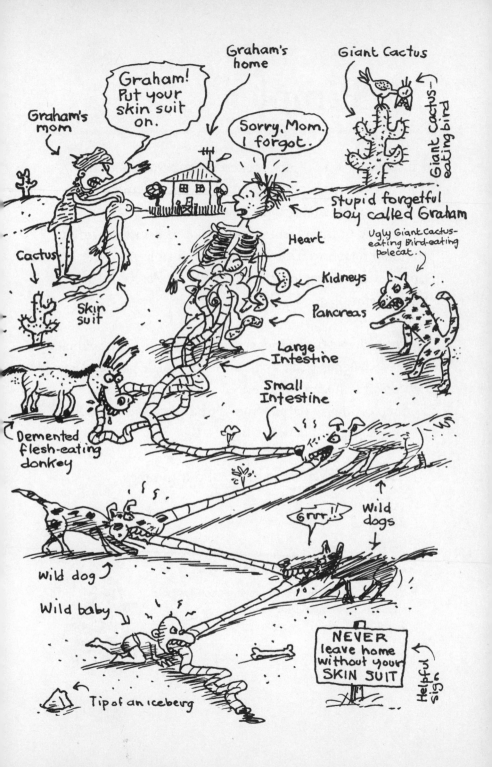

16. Pimples

Pimples are small, pus-packed protuberances that appear mostly on people's faces and necks and sometimes on their posteriors.

Pimple-popping is a popular pastime and provided the inspiration for the well-known pimple-popping poem "Peter Pimple-popper Popped a Patch of Pus-packed Pimples."

> Peter Pimple-popper popped a patch of pus-packed pimples
> A patch of pus-packed pimples Peter Pimple-popper popped.
> If Peter Pimple-popper popped a patch of pus-packed pimples, where's the pus from the pus-packed pimples Peter Pimple-popper popped?

That is all there is to know about pimples.

A&T'S FUN BODY PART FACT #16

Pimples were invented in 1949 by the deranged criminal mastermind Count Von Acne.

Count Von Acne

17. Scabs

Scabs are dried crusts of blood that form over a wound while it heals. They are highly prized by scab collectors, who search for them using electronic scab-detectors, and regularly trade for millions of dollars on internet scab-trading sites such as eScab and Scabazon.com.

The world's largest scab museum has a collection of over ten million scabs, some dating as far back as the Stone Age, and is well worth a visit if you like looking at old, dried-up crusts of blood.

That is all there is to know about scabs.

A&T'S FUN BODY PART FACT #17

Scabs are called "scabs" because they look like scabs.

18. Freckles

Freckles are not as dangerous as everybody seems to think they are.

While it is true that over 2,000 people die each year in freckle attacks, these occur mostly as a result of severe provocation.

Freckles are, on the whole, peaceful and quite shy creatures. If you leave them alone, they'll leave you alone.

That is all there is to know about freckles.

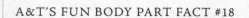

A&T'S FUN BODY PART FACT #18

People who have freckles get really sick of people who don't have freckles saying to them, "You know, if all your freckles joined up, you'd actually have a really good tan."

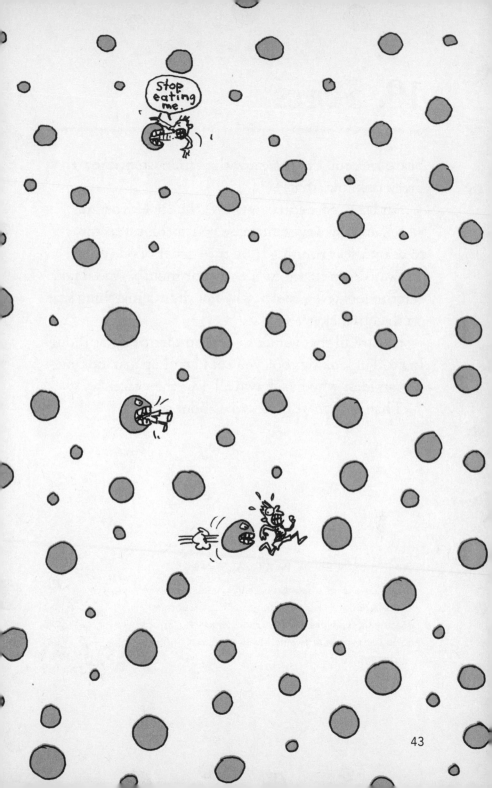

43

19. Scars

Scars are cool. Pirates know that. Gangsters know that. *Everyone* knows that.

And the more scars you have, the cooler you are.

So, an easy way to increase your coolness factor is to draw a scar running from the corner of one eye all the way down to the corner of your mouth. And if you want to look even cooler, why not draw a matching scar on the other side?

Be careful that you don't get too carried away, though. Instead of looking cool, you could end up just looking like an idiot who has drawn all over their face.

That is all there is to know about scars.

A&T'S FUN BODY PART FACT #19

Many fictional characters have scars. Some of the most famous are Harry Potter (forehead), Captain Hook (cheek), Frankenstein's monster (neck), Freddy Krueger (everywhere), and Madeline (lower right abdomen).

Even A&T's fun body part fact #19 has a cool scar.

YOUR SKIN:
An amazing cross section

If you think skin is just boring old skin, then think again. You have three layers of skin and every square centimeter contains thousands of cells and hundreds of sweat glands, oil glands, nerve endings, blood vessels, lost submarines, monster-chickens, anvils, cactuses, kittens, puppies, ponies, and a whole bunch of other stuff that you never would have guessed.

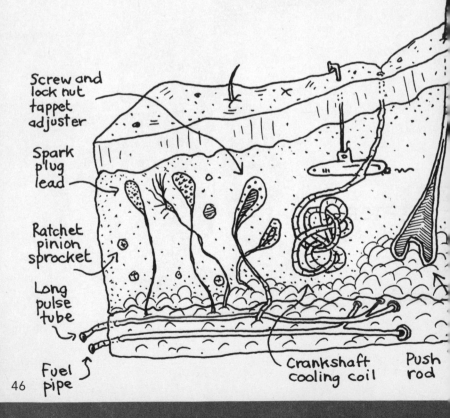

Screw and lock nut tappet adjuster

Spark plug lead

Ratchet pinion sprocket

Long pulse tube

Fuel pipe

Crankshaft cooling coil

Push rod

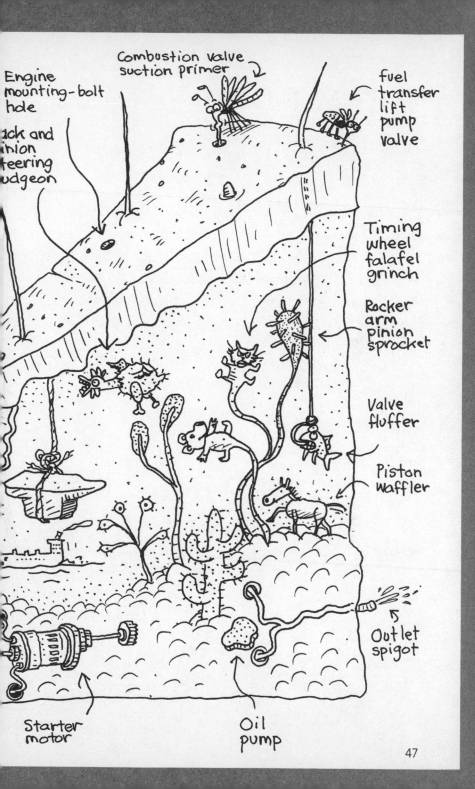

Combustion valve
suction primer

Engine
mounting-bolt
hole

ack and
inion
teering
udgeon

fuel
transfer
lift
pump
valve

Timing
wheel
falafel
grinch

Rocker
arm
pinion
sprocket

Valve
fluffer

Piston
Waffler

Outlet
spigot

Starter
motor

Oil
pump

47

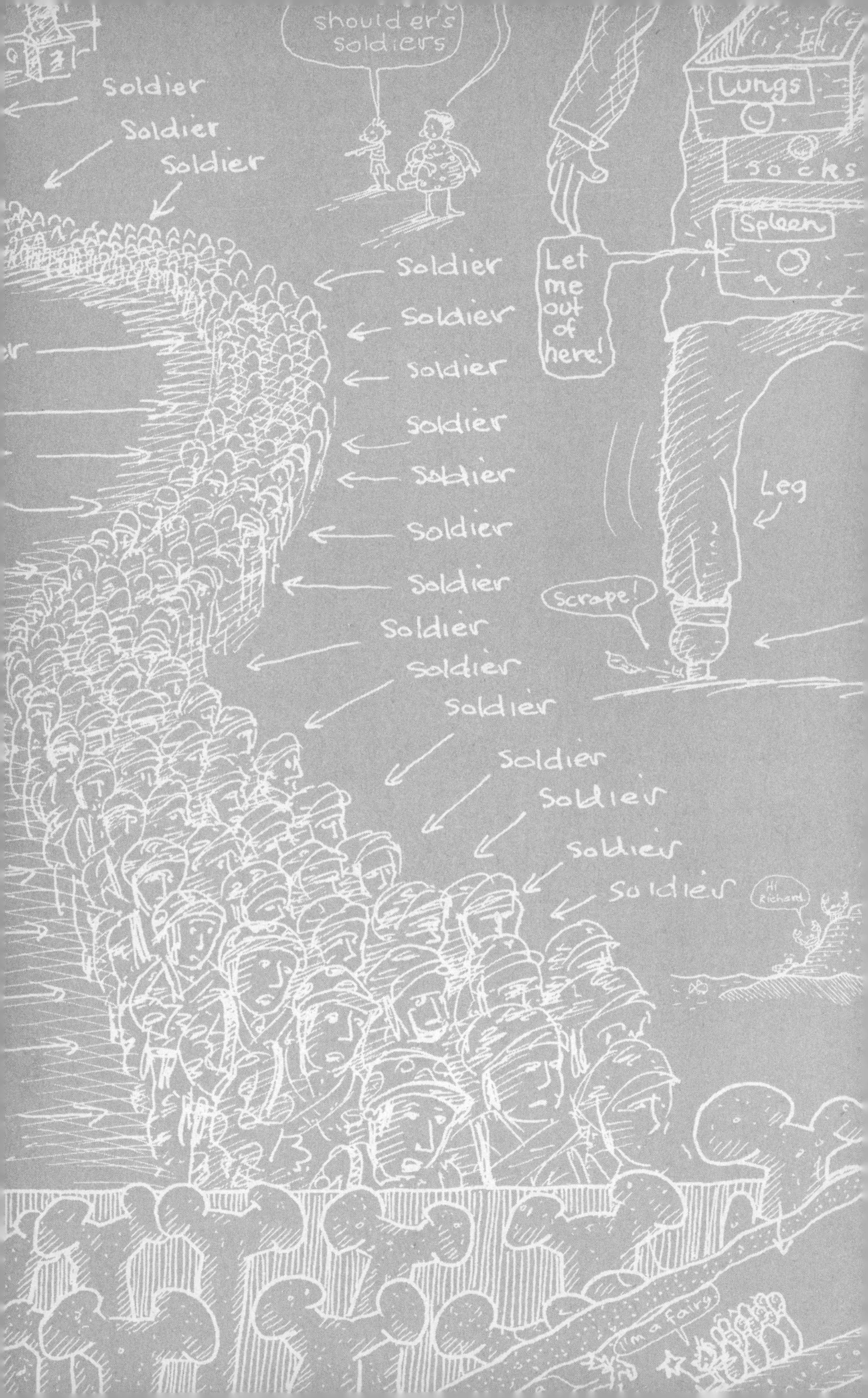
shoulder's soldiers
Soldier
Soldier
Soldier
Lungs
Socks
Spleen
Let me out of here!
Soldier
Soldier
Soldier
Soldier
Soldier
Soldier
Soldier
Leg
Scrape!
Soldier
Soldier
Soldier
Soldier
Soldier
Soldier
Soldier
Hi Richard
I'm a fairy

SECTION 3

Upper Body

Your upper body is right below your neck and right above your bottom. Here is everything there is to know about your upper body.

20. Shoulders

Your shoulders are located directly beneath your ears.

Their main function is to help you avoid answering difficult questions. You do this by raising and dropping your shoulders rapidly: This is called "shrugging." Examples of the difficult sorts of questions that I'm talking about are: Who broke that? Who made that mess? Why is your sister crying? Why isn't the dog breathing? How did the goldfish get in the toaster?

If you are ever asked questions like these, you have the right to remain silent. Just shrug. It may also help if you raise your eyebrows at the same time. If this doesn't work, then run (*see* LEGS, page 74).

That is all there is to know about shoulders.

A&T'S FUN BODY PART FACT #20

Shoulders are the body part most commonly mispronounced as "soldiers."

I am a shoulder.

21. Chest

Your chest is on the top half of the front of your body and is a handy place to keep your ribs, your heart, and your lungs.

Your chest is also an ideal place to hang medals, ribbons, and name tags, but be careful when pinning these onto your chest that you don't puncture your lungs with the pin or all the air will rush out and you will fly around the room like a balloon without its end tied.

That is all there is to know about chests.

A&T'S FUN BODY PART FACT #21

Pirates like to put their stolen treasure in wooden chests and bury them on deserted islands.

My chest's not Wooden!!

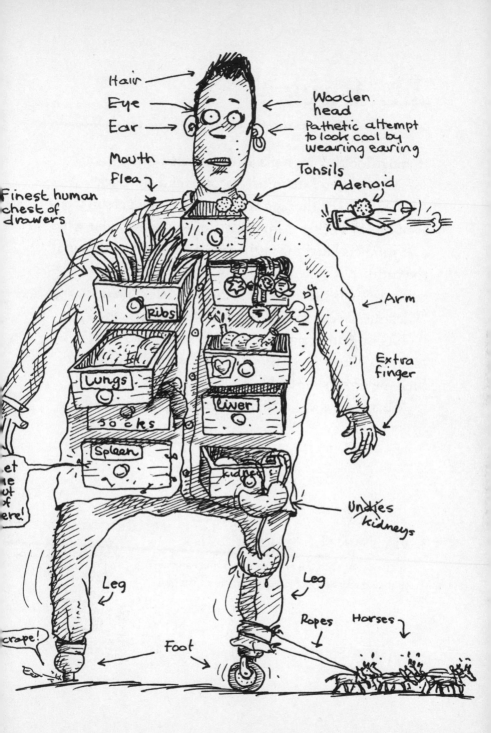

53

22. Back

If you're looking for a place to stick a funny sign on somebody, then I definitely recommend the back.

If you attach the sign very carefully, the person won't even know it's there. They may, of course, wonder why everybody is laughing at them but that only makes it all the funnier.

Funny signs to stick on someone's back include: "Kick me," "Kiss me," and "Kick me and kiss me."

Not-so-funny signs to stick on someone's back include: "Don't kick me," "Don't kiss me," and "Don't kick me or kiss me or I'll tell my mommy."*

That is all there is to know about backs.

A&T'S FUN BODY PART FACT #22

Human beings are the only mammals that can sleep on their backs (without looking completely stupid).

*Yeah, I know . . . this one is a *little* bit funny.

23. Arms

Arms are the long, arm-shaped things that stick out of your shoulders and hold your hands on.

Many famous people throughout history have had arms.

Neil Armstrong used his arms to plant a flag on the moon.

Jimi Hendrix used his arms to play awesome guitar.

Mary Shelley used her arms—well, at least one of them—to write her famous novel, *Frankenstein*, in which the scientist Dr. Frankenstein uses his arms to build a creature out of body parts stolen from dead bodies—including arms.

Dr. Frankenstein later comes to regret creating his monster because it uses *its* arms to kill people.

So, as you can see, you can use your arms for good or evil: The choice is yours.

That is all there is to know about arms.

A&T'S FUN BODY PART FACT #23

The span of your outstretched arms—from fingertip to fingertip—is the same as your height.

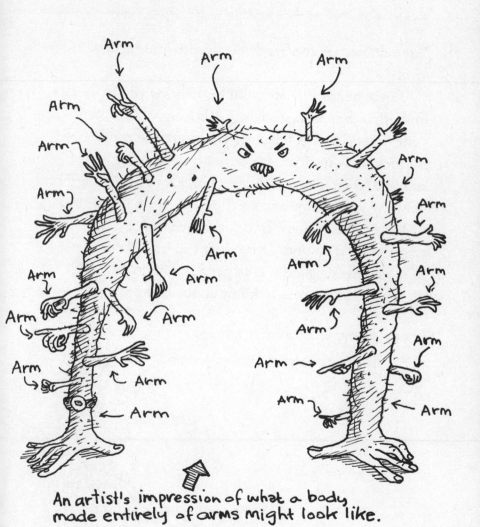

An artist's impression of what a body made entirely of arms might look like.

24. Elbows

Your elbows are the bendy bits in the middle of your arms.

These bendy bits are good for helping you to do lots of stuff, like saluting, waving, drinking, and picking your nose. (Note: Obviously you don't use your elbow for picking your nose—your fingers are much better suited to the purpose—but try to pick your nose *without* bending your elbow and you'll soon see what I mean.)

Jabbing your elbow into someone is a good way to get their attention. Don't do it too hard, however, because that's a good way to get a punch in the face.

That is all there is to know about elbows.

A&T'S FUN BODY PART FACT #24

It is physically impossible to lick your own elbow.

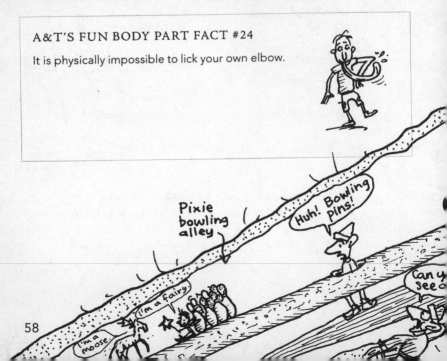

Pixie bowling alley

Huh! Bowling pins!

I'm a fairy

I'm a moose

Can y see o

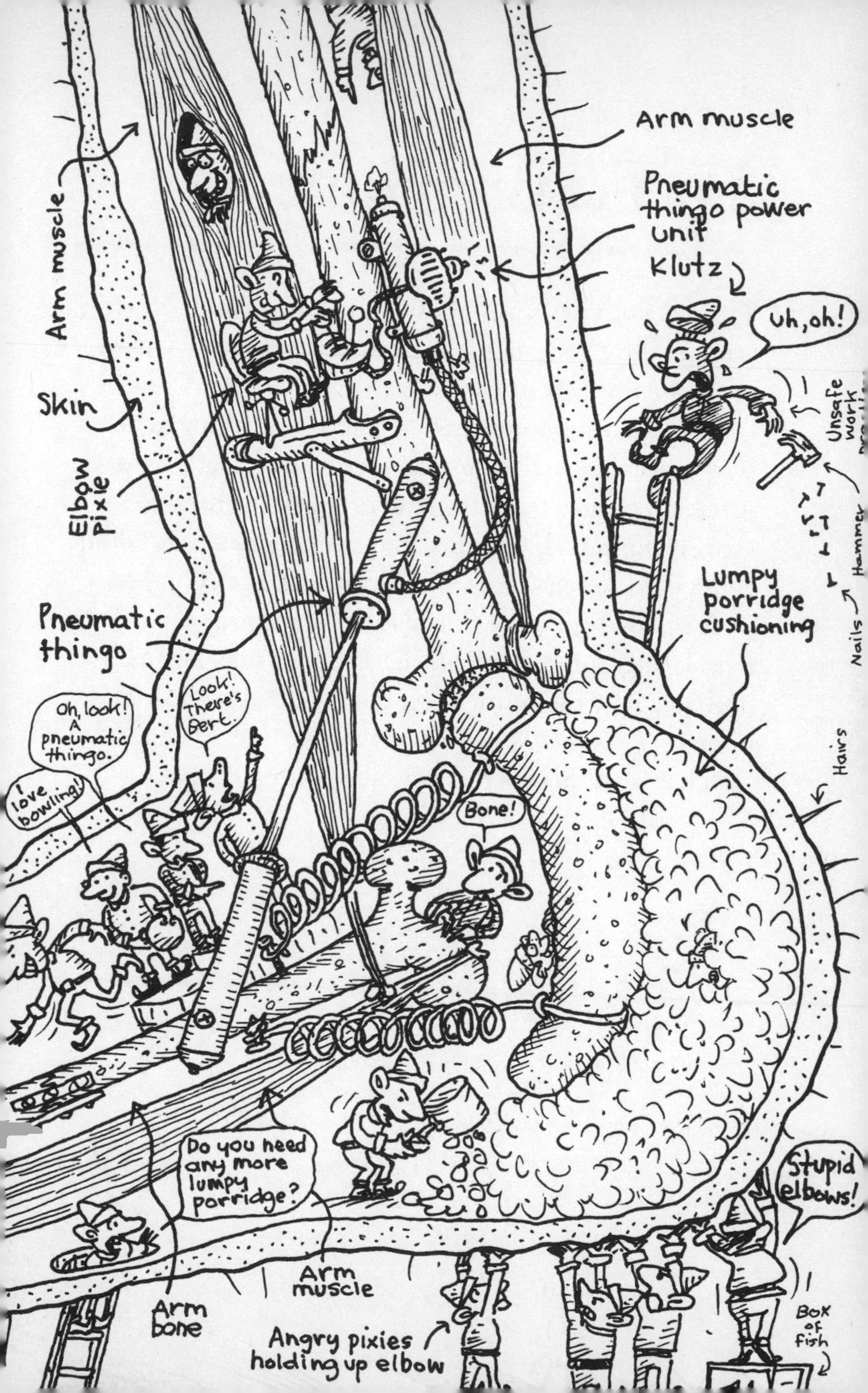
Arm muscle
Pneumatic thingo power unit
Klutz
Uh, oh!
Unsafe work
Hammer
Nails
Arm muscle
Skin
Elbow pixie
Pneumatic thingo
Lumpy porridge cushioning
Oh, look! A pneumatic thingo.
Look! There's Bert.
I love bowling!
Hairs
Bone!
Do you need any more lumpy porridge?
Stupid elbows!
Arm muscle
Arm bone
Angry pixies holding up elbow
Box of fish

25. Funny Bone

There is nothing funny about your funny bone, which is not really a bone at all, but a nerve that lies very close to the skin near your elbow.

You can test out just how *unfunny* your funny bone is by whacking your funny bone on the edge of a hard surface. You may feel pain. You may feel the need to express this pain by yelping, screaming, or cursing—but you will definitely not feel like laughing.

It is, however, quite funny to see somebody *else* whack their funny bone on the edge of a table, which is probably how the funny bone got its name in the first place.

That is all there is to know about funny bones.

A&T'S FUN BODY PART FACT #25

More people are killed annually by donkeys than die in air crashes. (This has nothing to do with the funny bone, but it is kind of funny.)

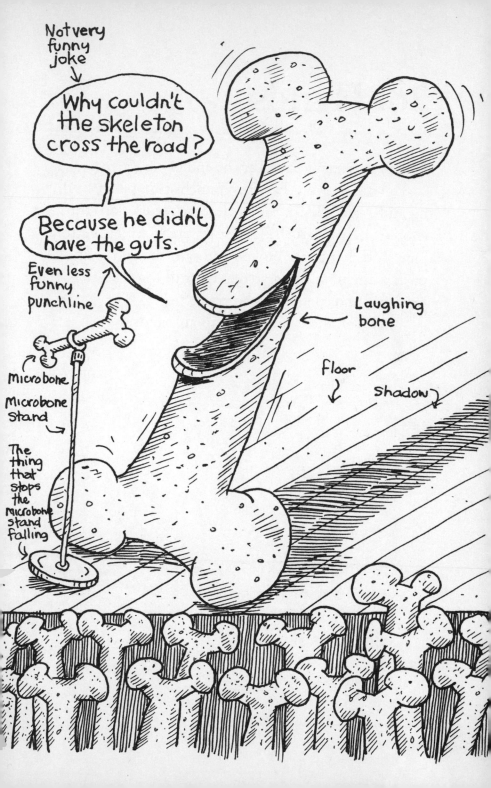

26. Hands

Hands are usually found at the end of your arms.

You can use your hands to punch stuff, pinch stuff, hit stuff, stroke stuff, pat stuff, smack stuff, slap stuff, chop stuff, paint stuff, make stuff, break stuff, fix stuff, hide stuff that you've broken and can't fix, pull stuff, push stuff, lift stuff, scratch itchy stuff, wash stuff, dry stuff, and conduct orchestras.

That is all there is to know about hands.

A&T'S FUN BODY PART FACT #26

One hundred percent of all humans agree that the scariest thing in the world is a severed hand crawling across the floor towards your bed in the middle of the night.

Skeleton

Tie

Victim ↓

host →

loset ↘

evered
hand ↘

lime ↘

← floor

Shadow ↑

Blood ↗

Page
number ↙

63

27. Fingers

Fingers are generally found hanging off the ends of your hands and are good for a whole range of things, mostly beginning with the letter "P," such as poking, pointing, piano-playing, picking posies, picking noses, pinching, prodding, pushing buttons, and making peace signs, just to name a few.

Despite their usefulness, fingers are quite shy and can often be found attempting to hide the tips of themselves in your nostrils.

That is all there is to know about fingers.

A&T'S FUN BODY PART FACT #27

The fingerprints of koala bears are virtually indistinguishable from those of humans, so much so that they could be confused for human fingerprints at a crime scene.

Hee, hee!

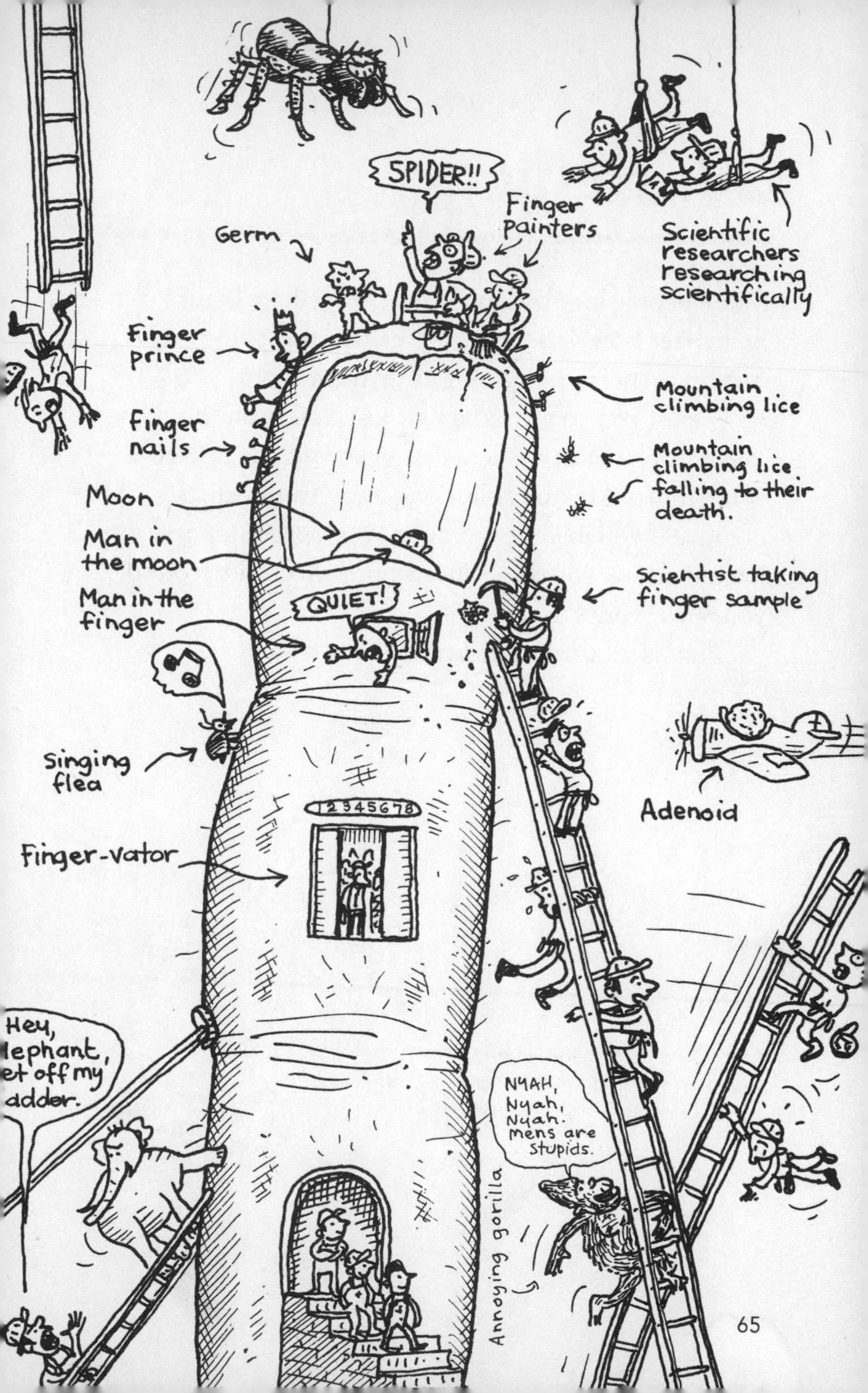

SPIDER!!
Germ
Finger painters
Scientific researchers researching scientifically
Finger prince
Mountain climbing lice
Finger nails
Mountain climbing lice falling to their death.
Moon
Man in the moon
Man in the finger
QUIET!
Scientist taking finger sample
Singing flea
12345678
Adenoid
Finger-vator
Hey, lephant, et off my adder.
NYAH, Nyah, Nyah. mens are stupids.
Annoying gorilla

28. Belly

Some people love bellies. Some people hate bellies. But no matter how you feel about bellies, one thing is for certain—there's no getting away from them.

Even if you went to the loneliest desert on the loneliest planet in the loneliest galaxy in the universe, you still wouldn't be able to get away from bellies, because if you just zipped open your space suit and looked down, you'd see one right there on the front of your own body!

That is all there is to know about bellies.

A&T'S FUN BODY PART FACT #28

Gut-barging is a sport in which two overweight contestants try to barge each other off a large mat using their big fat bellies.

29. Belly Button

Your belly button is located in the middle of your belly.

Belly buttons are useful markers to show how high to pull your pants up, as well as being great for stopping the uncontrolled spread of belly fluff.

The best thing about belly buttons, though, is that without them, you'd be walking around attached to your mother for the rest of your life.

Depending on the type of mother you have, this could stop you from being able to do a lot of the things that you like, such as riding on roller coasters, watching scary movies and, of course, complaining to your friends about your mother.

That is all there is to know about belly buttons.

A&T'S FUN BODY PART FACT #29

The Japanese city of Shibukawa holds an annual Belly Button Festival. People dance in the streets with faces painted on their stomachs.

Innie

Outie

Fluffy

Spiral outie

Angry outie

Nose-picking outie

AMAZING THINGS PEOPLE CAN DO WITH THEIR BODIES

Over the many thousands of years that people have had bodies, they have worked out many amazing things to do with them.

This is Agnetha Squelch. Agnetha can make funny noises using her hand and her armpit. See how Agnetha delights her family and friends with her rare and special talent.

This is Felicity Drool. Felicity can amuse herself for hours by staring into a mirror and curling her tongue into a little tube.

Brilliant!

This is Richard Horrible. Richard survived for three years on a desert island eating nothing but his own earwax. Luckily, it came in two different flavors—left ear and right ear—so he didn't get bored.

This is Le Petomane, a French flatuist, who entertained thousands of people with his professional farting. Highlights of his act included impressions of cannon fire, thunderstorms, and the 1906 San Francisco earthquake.

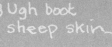

SECTION 4

Lower Body

Your lower body starts at the ground,
goes up to your bottom, and all the way back
down again. Here is everything there is to
know about your lower body.

30. Legs

Your legs start at the top of the ground and go all the way up until they reach the bottom of your bottom and then they go all the way back down until they reach the top of the ground again.

You can use your legs to walk from the bottom of a hill to the top of a hill. You can also use them to walk from the top of the hill back down to the bottom again.

Legs are also useful if you need to run away from anything or anyone—for example, somebody asking difficult questions you'd rather not answer (*see* SHOULDERS, page 50).

That is all there is to know about legs.

A&T'S FUN BOD

In 1836, Mexican Ger held an elaborate sta his amputated leg.

Doppel-ganger

Grankel bankel doppelganger

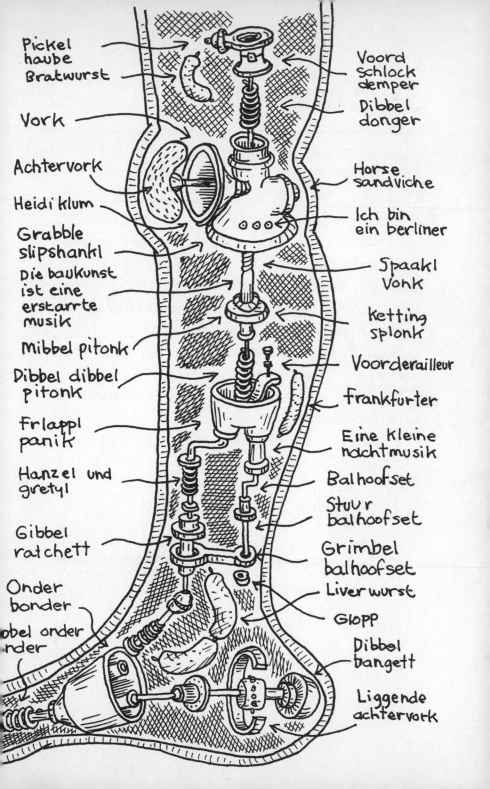

31. Butt

(ALSO KNOWN AS BUTTOCKS, BUM, BOTTOM)

The butt is located on the back of the body at the top of the legs. It is generally agreed that butts have the worst job on the human body. Not only do they have to do all the dirty work, but they get no respect. They get kicked, smacked, laughed at, and sat on. They never get to see anything or watch television because they're trapped in people's underpants all day long.

Butts are very envious of heads because heads get to ride around on top of people's necks and butts would like nothing better than to swap places with them, by force if necessary.

History is littered with tales of butt uprisings led by rebel butts intent on improving their position on the human body.

That is all there is to know about butts.

A&T'S FUN BODY PART FACT #31

The Day My Butt Went Psycho, the tale of a runaway butt that tries to take over the world, is based on a true story.

32. Thighs

Thighs are nice, big, juicy, upper-leg muscles that are very good for eating if, say, you've been lost at sea for many days and you're starving.

You wouldn't eat your own thighs, of course; that would be stupid.

If you're hungry, always eat somebody else's thighs, but remember to spit out the leg bones and avoid the butt because not only do butts not taste very nice, when you are rescued and everybody asks how you survived, you'll have to tell them all that you ate somebody's butt, which will be very embarrassing.

That is all there is to know about thighs.

A&T'S FUN BODY PART FACT #32

Poets love the word "thigh" because it rhymes with lots of other words, such as: hi, guy, cry, fly, high, spy, try, die, sky, tie, and bye-bye.

33. Calves

Calves are really sweet.

Calves are really cute.

Calves are really sweet and really cute. The muscles in your lower leg are called calves. But they are not as sweet and cute as real calves.

That is all there is to know about calves.

A&T'S FUN BODY PART FACT #33

Calves are the larval form of cows.

34. Ankles

Ankles are the bendy bit where the foot and leg meet.

Without ankles, we wouldn't have ankle sprain, ankle strain, ankle socks, ankle bracelets, ankle-strap shoes, ankle tattoos, ankle-biters, ankle-dusters, or Anklyosaurs.

Actually, anklyosaurs have nothing to do with ankles, I just like the name.

That is all there is to know about ankles.

A&T'S FUN BODY PART FACT #34

A fear of ankles is called *anklephobia*. A fear of catching anklephobia is called *anklephobia-phobia*.

35. Feet

Feet. We've all got them (except for people without feet) and we all need them (except for people without legs) and we all use them to get from place to place (except for people who drive everywhere) and we all know they get a bit stinky (except for people who change their socks at least twice a day) and we all say rude words if we drop a fridge on them (except for really careful people who manage to get through their whole lives without ever dropping a fridge on their foot).

That is all there is to know about feet.

A&T'S FUN BODY PART FACT #35

A pair of human feet contains 250,000 sweat glands and is home to about two trillion bacteria. So, the only thing worse than having to kiss someone on the lips would be having to kiss them on the feet (see LIPS, page 20).

Legs →

Feet

Bacteria diving board

Jell
ba

Old dry bit of carrot

Chicken bone →

HB Pencil

Cork →

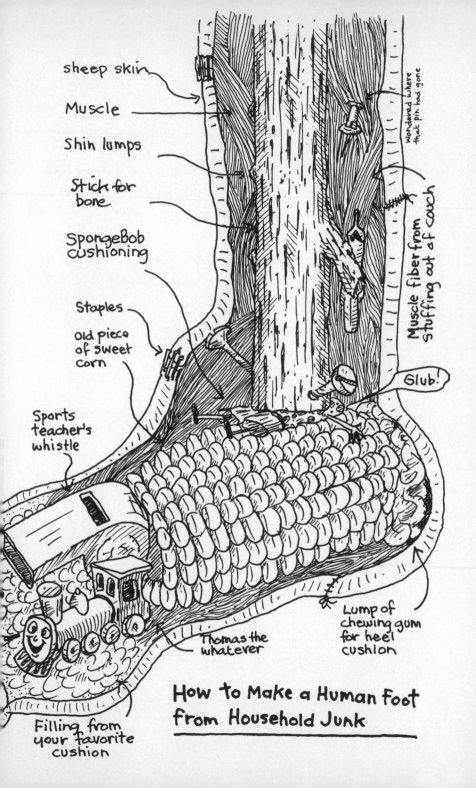

sheep skin

Muscle

Shin lumps

Stick for bone

SpongeBob cushioning

Staples

Old piece of sweet corn

Sports teacher's whistle

Wondered where that pin had gone

Muscle fiber from stuffing out of couch

Glub!

Lump of chewing gum for heel cushion

Thomas the whatever

Filling from your favorite cushion

How to Make a Human Foot from Household Junk

36. Toes

Toes are the short, wiggly things on the end of your feet. Some go to market, some stay home, some have roast beef, and some have none, and some go, "Wee! Wee! Wee!" all the way home.

That is all there is to know about toes.

A&T'S FUN BODY PART FACT #36

Jack Daniel—the man who invented Jack Daniel's whisky—kicked his office safe in a temper one day and ended up with an infected toe, which killed him. If only he'd put his toe in his own whisky to kill the germs, he would have been cured!

THE GREAT HUMAN BODY EXPEDITION OF 1858

In 1858, a group of scientists miniaturized themselves and launched an expedition into the insides of a human body. Nothing of any lasting value was learned, but all agreed it was a great day out. The accompanying picture is an artist's reconstruction of what the expedition might have looked like, based both on eyewitness and completely made-up accounts.

PART 2

The Parts You Can't See

Dyna Thr

Bit of
sponge

Teeth

Eye

Life
vests

Grapes

Avacado

Bananas

SECTION 5

Musculoskeletal System

Muscles aren't much use without a skeleton to hang them off. And a skeleton isn't much use without muscles to hold it up and make it go. Here is everything there is to know about the musculoskeletal system.

37. Skeleton

There are three important things to know about skeletons.

The first is that skeletons are really scary.

The second is that they are everywhere! Pretty much any time you're in a graveyard after midnight, you'll get chased by them, and every time you open a closet in a haunted house, one will jump out at you.

Sure, I know what you're thinking . . . you're thinking, "Well, I'll just keep away from graveyards after midnight and I won't open closet doors in haunted houses and I'll be safe."

But you're wrong because the third thing—and the scariest thing of all—is that there is a skeleton inside you right now and there is *nothing* you can do about it!

That is all there is to know about skeletons.

A&T'S FUN BODY PART FACT #37

The most painful operation you can possibly have is a complete skeleton transplant.

Hmmm! Doesn't look quite right.

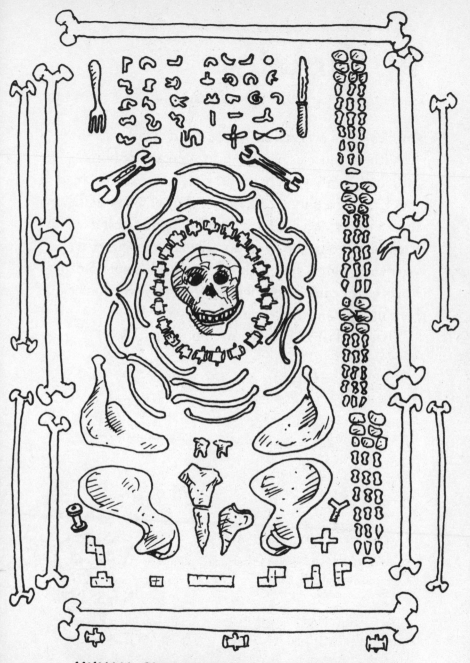

HUMAN SKELETON D.I.Y. KIT (206 parts)

38. Muscles

Muscles make everything in your body work.

Without muscles, you couldn't run, jump, blink, sniff, kick, swim, punch, point, kiss, frown, smile, read a book, make a phone call, have a shower, go bowling, climb a tree, ride a bike, eat a hamburger, digest a hamburger, go to the bathroom, swat a mosquito, write your name, light a fire, pick a flower, and about 75 other things that I can't be bothered writing down because the muscles in my fingers are getting tired.

That is all there is to know about muscles.

A&T'S FUN BODY PART FACT #38

Your body uses 300 muscles to balance itself when you are standing still.

MUSCLE MATCH-UP

(a) Reading a book (b) Making a phone call
(c) Having a shower (d) Bowling (e) Punching
(f) Climbing a tree (g) Riding a bike (h) Kicking
(i) Going to the bathroom (j) swimming
(k) Pointing (j) Jumping

39. Tendons

If you think that muscles are cool and tendons are dumb, then you are definitely wrong.

Tendons connect your muscles to your bones.

You could have the biggest muscles in the world, but without tendons, you'd be weaker than the weakest weakling on Earth.

Without tendons, you wouldn't even be able to get out of bed. In fact, you'd be so weak you wouldn't be able to get *into* bed in the first place. You'd just lie there on the bedroom floor, wishing you had tendons to join your muscles to your bones.

That is all there is to know about tendons.

A&T'S FUN BODY PART FACT #39

When you rearrange the letters of a word to make a new word, it's called an "anagram." An anagram of "tendon" is "denton" and Terry Denton is the illustrator of this book! And he has lots of tendons! Anagrams are spooky!

Dyna Thriffigs
Anagram of Andy Griffiths

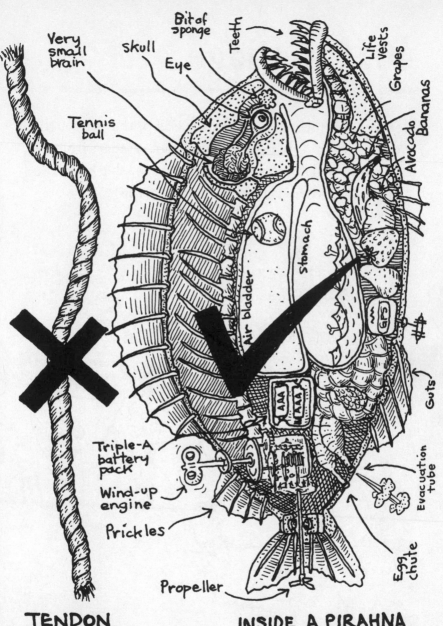

TENDON
Like a bit of string
(VERY BORING)

INSIDE A PIRAHNA
(VERY INTERESTING !!)

40. Cartilage

Nothing is known about cartilage except that it's tough and rubbery and sharks are made from it (apart from their teeth, which are made of 100 percent shark tooth).

That is all there is to know about cartilage.

A&T'S FUN BODY PART FACT #40

Cartilage is tough and rubbery and sharks are made from it.

HOW TO WALK IN 15 EASY STEPS

Walking is not as easy as it might seem. It requires the coordination of many parts of your body all at the same time. Here is a simple guide to help you get to where you want to go.

1. Start with your hands by your side.

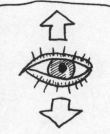

2. Ensure your eyes are open.

3. Use your eyes to check the path ahead is clear.

4. Lift your right foot off the ground.

5. Move your right foot forward.

6. Move your left arm forward.

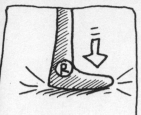

7. Place your right foot down on the ground.

8. Lift your left foot off the ground.

9. Bring your left arm back.

10. Move your right arm forward.

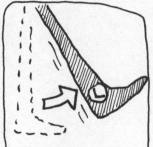

11. Move your left foot forward.

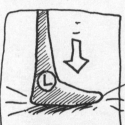

12. Place your left foot down on the ground.

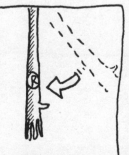

13. Bring your right arm back.

14. Repeat steps 4 to 13 until you reach your destination.

15. Stop.

Head & Throat

Have you ever wondered what's going on behind your face? Here is everything there is to know about the inside of your head and throat.

41. Brain

The human brain has 12 billion brain cells, which, when you think about it, is an awful lot of thinking power.

Unfortunately, not all of the 12 billion brain cells actually work at the same time, which explains why so many people with 12 billion brain cells of thinking power push doors marked PULL, pull doors marked PUSH, step in puddles, step in dog poo, and give themselves brain freeze by drinking Slurpees too fast.

That is all there is to know about brains.

A&T'S FUN BODY PART FACT #41

Terry Denton doesn't actually have a brain. I once shone a torch into his ear while he was asleep and I couldn't see a thing.

Andy

Torch

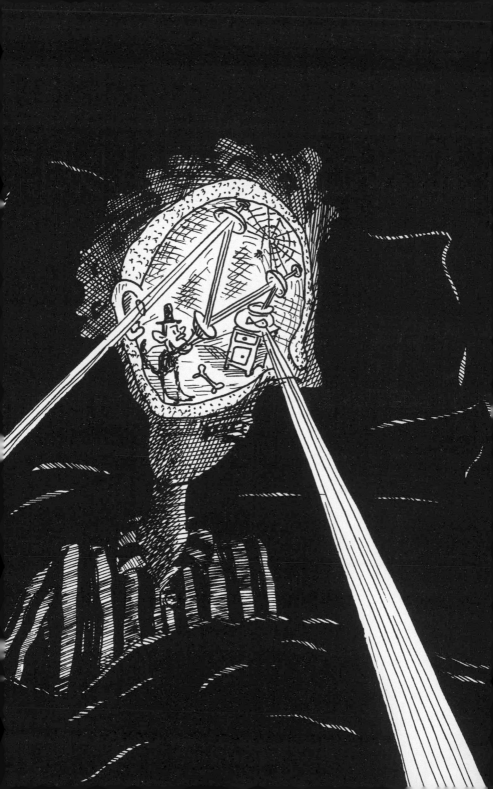

42. Nervous System

The nervous system is made up of a complicated bunch of nerves that carry messages from the brain to the body and back again. Every second, each nerve cell in your brain receives over 100,000 messages. The following edited transcript of a few moments in the life of the nervous system gives you an idea of just how much pressure it's under. "Blink! Breathe! Eat! Stop eating! Digest food! Burp! Apologize! Drink! Stop drinking! Empty bladder! Blink! Breathe! Empty bladder! Scratch bottom! Pick nose! Not with the same finger, you idiot! And for goodness sakes, EMPTY YOUR BLADDER! NOW!!!"

Phew, that's a lot of stuff to take care of. No wonder the nervous system is so nervous.

That is all there is to know about nervous systems.

A&T'S FUN BODY PART FACT #42

There are more nerve cells in your body than there are stars in the Milky Way.

...1,200,066, 1,200,067, 1,200,068...

43. Spinal Cord

Spinal Cord were a stupid heavy metal band that sang songs exclusively about the nervous system.

One of the band's biggest hits was "Salival Stimulation," from their 1974 album *Sympathetic Ganglia*.

This was followed by a string of hits, including "Pupil Dilator," "Heart Accelerator," "Glucose Stimulator" and "Bladder Contractor" from their *Thoracic Park* double album.

The band eventually broke up in 1976, citing musical differences—some band members wanted to continue exploring the nervous system while others wanted to branch out and sing about hands, feet, and other appendages.

That is all there is to know about Spinal Cord.

A&T'S FUN BODY PART FACT #43

The organ most featured in popular songs is the heart, for example: "Achy Breaky Heart," "Groove Is in the Heart," "Your Cheatin' Heart." The least represented organ is the gallbladder, with only three known songs in its honor—all by Spinal Cord.

Gallbladder

111

44. Throat

Your throat connects your mouth with your stomach, and your lungs with your air supply.

When my grandfather had a sore throat, he used to treat it by mixing a teaspoon of gravel into a glass of whisky and drinking it. He said it worked because the germs got drunk on the whisky and then had a rock fight with the gravel and killed each other. My grandfather got a *lot* of sore throats.

That is all there is to know about throats (and my grandfather).

A&T'S FUN BODY PART FACT #44

The art of inserting swords, bayonets, and neon tubes down your throat is called sword swallowing. It takes three to seven years to learn, and a further five years to master this extremely dangerous skill.

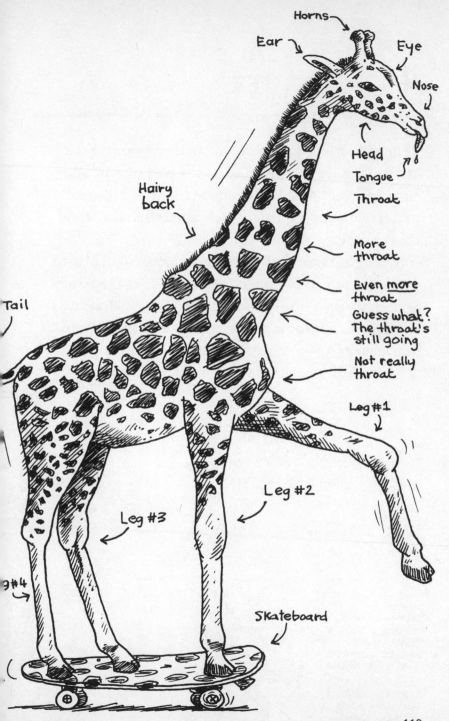

Horns

Ear

Eye

Nose

Head

Tongue

Throat

Hairy
back

More
throat

Even **more**
throat

Tail

Guess what?
The throat's
still going

Not really
throat

Leg #1

Leg #2

Leg #3

9 #4

Skateboard

113

45. Larynx

Your larynx is in your throat. Another name for the larynx is "voice box" because it's the part of your body that makes it possible for you to talk.

Humans are some of the few animals in the world that can talk.

Other animals that can talk are parrots, cockatoos, cartoon animals, talking horses, and I once read a news article in the *Northern Territory Times* about a cat that could swear. (It could say seven different swear words, which is pretty impressive for a cat.)

That is all there is to know about larynxes.

A&T'S FUN BODY PART FACT #45

If you can read this, thank a teacher. If you can read it aloud, thank your larynx.

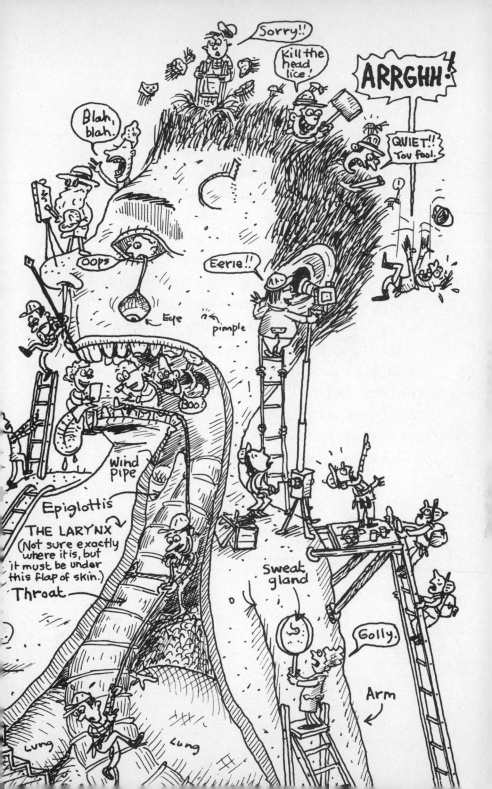

46. Epiglottis

If you want to be able to breathe and eat at the same time without choking, you're going to need an epiglottis.

To make an epiglottis, just take a piece of soft rubbery tissue and attach it to the roof of your tongue.

Position it in such a way that it points upward during breathing, but folds down flat when swallowing to stop food from going down into your windpipe.

But be careful and exercise common sense. If you insist on laughing and eating potato chips at the same time, not even the best homemade epiglottis in the world is going to save you from choking to death on a load of half-chewed chips.

That is all there is to know about epiglottises.

A&T'S FUN BODY PART FACT #46

The epiglottis was named after Epiglottis, an ancient Greek philosopher (341–270 BC) who invented potato chips, go-karts, and octopuses.

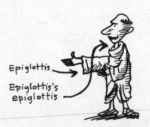

Epiglottis

Epiglottis's epiglottis

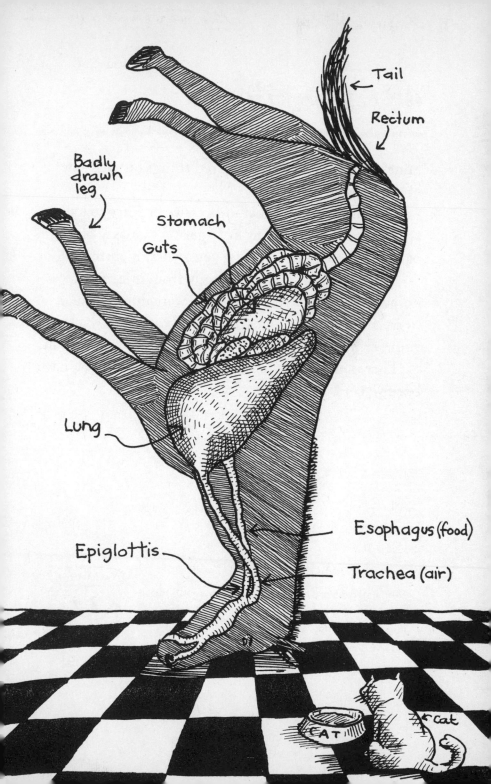

47. Tonsils

Your tonsils are those bunchy red things on each side of the back of your throat.

They might not be that impressive or scary to look at, but if you were a grimy little germ or a nasty bit of bacteria, these guys would be your worst nightmare.

Their job is to protect the body from infectious, no-good scum like you, and if you were dumb enough to try and get past them, they would catch you, kick your germy little butt, and bash your bacterial brains in.

That is all there is to know about tonsils . . . you have been warned.

A&T'S FUN BODY PART FACT #47

Human tonsils can bounce higher than a rubber ball of similar weight and size, but only for the first 30 minutes after they've been removed. After that, they're not much fun at all.

THE NATURAL DEFENSE SYSTEMS OF THE HUMAN BODY

There are many forms of self-defense, but these take many years of dedicated study to master. Not many people realize that their bodies come equipped with a variety of natural built-in defense systems that are surprisingly easy to use and very effective.

SPIT-BOXING
Closely related to kick-boxing, spit-boxing relies more on the power of the salivary ducts than the feet. Spit-boxing matches can take many hours and tend to go on until one of the opponents drowns.

PUS-KWON-DOE
Harnessing the power of a pus-packed pimple by pinching it until it pops is a surefire way to repel even the most determined attacker.

SPLAT!!

SNEEZE-POWERED MISSILES

A human sneeze can exceed
160 miles per hour.
The velocity enables it
to propel germs and
anything else you can
pack into your nostrils
up to 5 miles. Deadly over short ranges.

POO-JITSU

The ancient art of Poo-jitsu is as old as humanity itself.
It is one of the most unpleasant and smelliest forms of
self-defense ever invented,
except, perhaps, for SBDs.

SBDs

SBDs stands for "silent but deadlies."
They are one of the most unpleasant
and smelliest forms of self-defense
ever invented,
except, perhaps,
for Poo-jitsu.

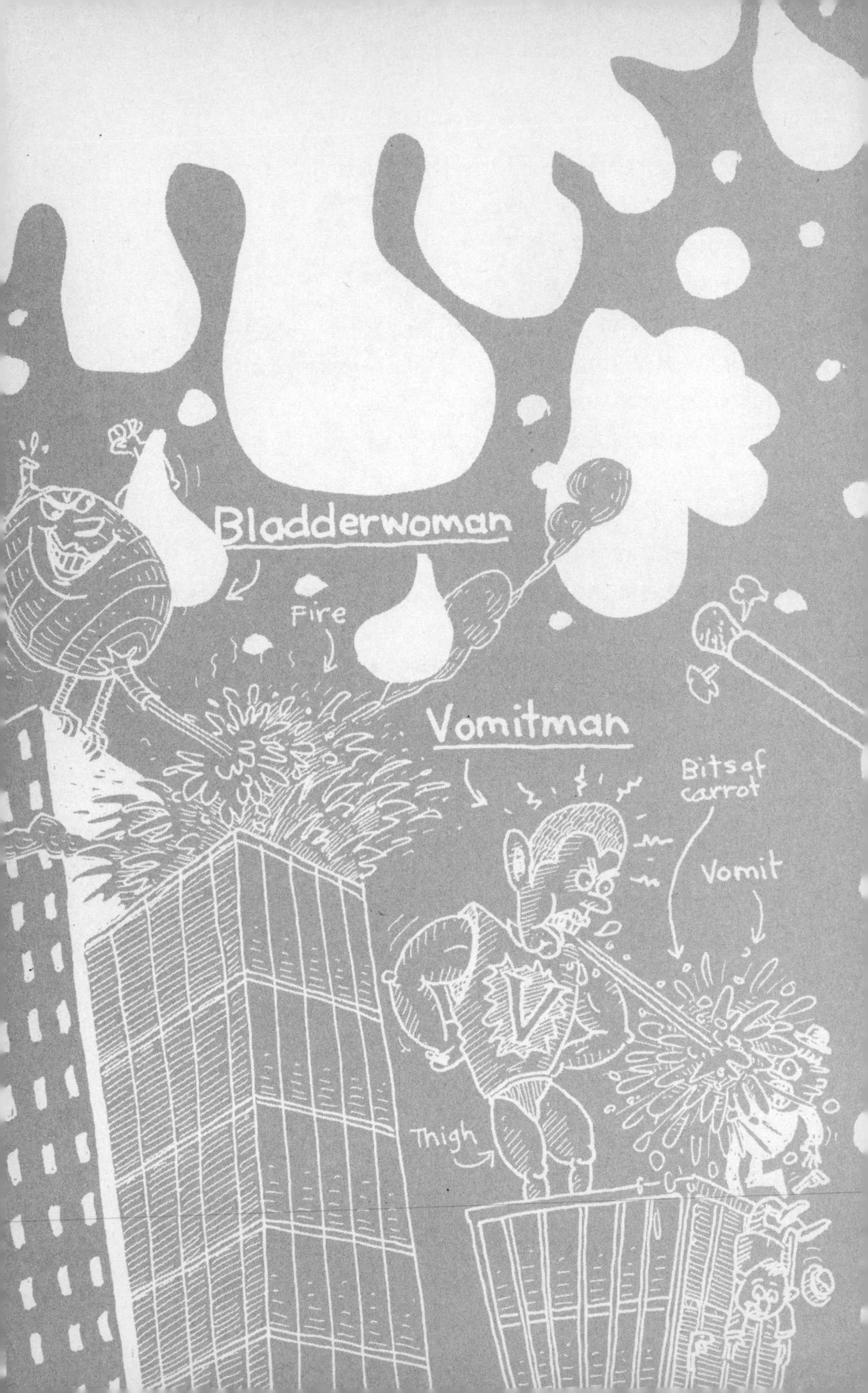

Bladderwoman
Fire
Vomitman
Bits of carrot
Vomit
Thigh

SECTION 7

Circulatory & Respiratory Systems

Your heart and lungs are the very heart and lungs of your body. Here is everything you need to know about the circulatory and respiratory systems.

48. Heart

Your heart beats from the moment you wake up till the moment you go to sleep.

It also beats from the moment you go to sleep till the moment you wake up again.

If you wake up and your heart is *not* beating, then you are probably dead. But don't worry too much about it. If you *are* dead, then you couldn't possibly have woken up, so whether or not you think your heart is beating, it probably is—in fact, even having the thought, "I wonder if my heart is beating?" means that your heart *must* be beating, otherwise you could never even have thought the thought!

That is all there is to know about hearts.

A&T'S FUN BODY PART FACT #48

Make your hand into a fist. That's how big your heart is. It is also how big your fist is.

I must be very bighearted!!

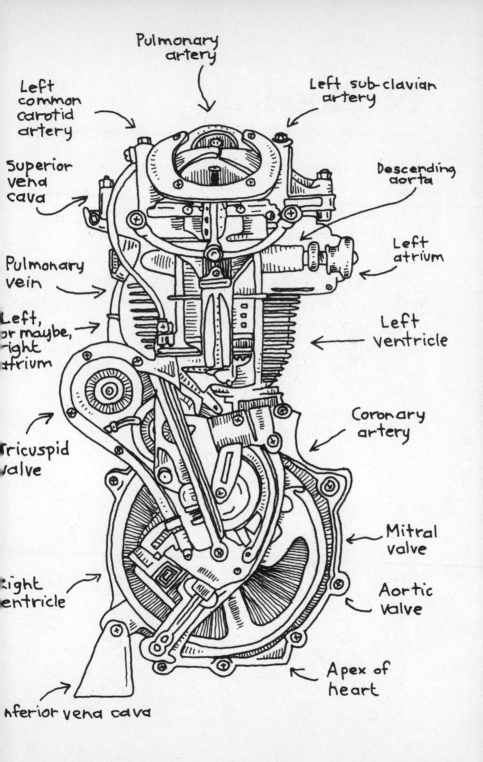

Pulmonary artery

Left sub-clavian artery

Left common carotid artery

Superior vena cava

Descending aorta

Left atrium

Pulmonary vein

Left, or maybe, right atrium

Left ventricle

Coronary artery

Tricuspid valve

Mitral valve

Right ventricle

Aortic valve

Apex of heart

Inferior vena cava

49. Blood

Blood is red and sticky and utterly essential for human life.

Without blood, we wouldn't have bloody noses, scabs, blood blisters, bruises, bloodshot eyes, Band-Aids, or vampires.

Vampires, of course, are not utterly essential for human life (if anything, they are the opposite), but I thought they should be included because they love blood and the thing they love most about it is sucking it hot and fresh straight out of your neck. So, if you've got a lot of blood in you, you should definitely watch out for vampires.

That is all there is to know about blood.

A&T'S FUN BODY PART FACT #49

There are approximately 160,000 miles of blood vessels in your body.

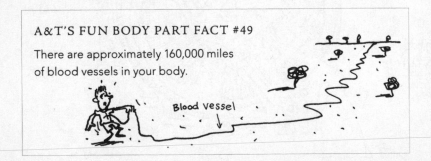

Blood vessel

Blood

127

50. Arteries

If you were to peel off all of your skin, you would see a complicated network of thin red tubes all over your body. These tubes are called arteries.

If you were to cut open one of these arteries, you would see a fountain of rich oxygenated blood spurt up into the air and all over the walls, the furniture, and the floor.

This would, of course, be entertaining, but ultimately a serious mistake because without a constant flow of rich oxygenated blood, many of your body's most important organs will begin shutting down within minutes and you will die.

That is all there is to know about arteries.

A&T'S FUN BODY PART FACT #50

Some people are so dumb that they actually *do* the things they read about. If you are one of these dumb people and just peeled off all your skin and cut one of the red tubes without realizing how dangerous this was, *see* VEINS, page 130.

Dumb person

skin

51. Veins

Just suppose you were reading a book called *What Body Part Is That?* and you got the crazy idea to peel off your skin and cut open one of the red tubes inside your body (*see* ARTERIES, page 128) and blood started spurting out all over the place, here's what you should do:

1. Start panicking: This is a really serious situation!
2. Stop panicking. See if you can identify a really complicated network of blue tubes—these are your veins and they carry de-oxygenated blood back to the heart.
3. Get all the blood that has spurted out of the red tube and shove it back into one of the blue tubes.
4. Tape up the artery, put your skin back on and never do anything so stupid ever again!
   That is all there is to know about veins.

A&T'S FUN BODY PART FACT #51

If you took all the veins in your body and put them end to end to make one giant vein, it would stretch 8,000 miles.

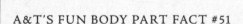

Or make a very big ball.

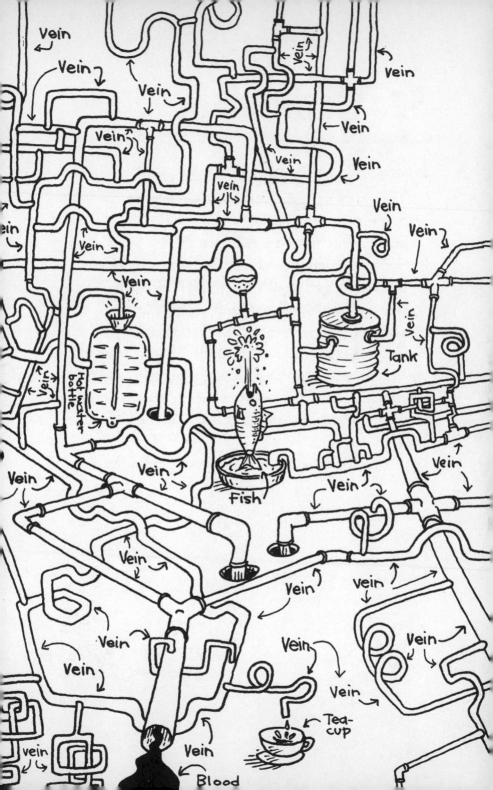

52. Capillaries

Capillaries are the larval form of butterflies.

They are soft and squishy and eat leaves.

Some are green and some are brown.

Some are hairy and some are smooth.

Some are friendly and cute and some spit poison.

But they are all capillaries and will one day make a cocoon out of silk and, through the amazing process of metamorphosis, turn into colorful butterflies.

Capillaries should not be confused with caterpillars, which, as we all know, form the connection between arteries and veins and assist in the exchange of gases, nutrients, and waste products between the blood and the tissue cells.

That is all there is to know about capillaries.

A&T'S FUN BODY PART FACT #52

Capillaries are the body part most commonly confused with caterpillars.

Caterpillar

It's not confusing.

I agree.

Capillary

53. Trachea

Another word for trachea is "windpipe."

Your trachea is the tube that leads from your mouth to your lungs.

You should keep your trachea free of blockages at all times in order to avoid choking to death. That is why it is a good idea *not* to swallow any—or all—of the following items: buttons, marbles, beads, coins, bottle caps, pen lids, pens, pencils, pencil sharpeners (manual or electric), golf balls, golf clubs, golf carts, shopping carts, elephants, or super-massive black holes that suck in everything around them including time and space itself.

That is all there is to know about tracheas.

A&T'S FUN BODY PART FACT #53

Black holes occur when a massive star goes supernova.

TAKE THE <u>TRACHEA TEST</u>.
Which things are safe to swallow?

Answer: None of them, you idiot!!

54. Lungs

Lungs are important because they help you breathe. Breathing is the fourth-most important thing you will *ever* do, right behind being born, dying, and having a cool hairstyle.

It's never too late to start breathing. Simply open your mouth, suck in a load of air, blow it all out again, and repeat for the rest of your life.

That is all there is to know about lungs.

A&T'S FUN BODY PART FACT #54

The name of the lung disease "pneumonoultramicroscopicsilicovolcanoconiosis" is the longest word in the English language. It is so long, in fact, that by the time a doctor has finished telling someone they have this disease, the unlucky person has usually died of old age.

BODY PART AND BODY PART–RELATED SUPERHEROES

Superheroes have long used their body parts and body part–related products to protect and serve the human race. Here are five of the greatest body part and body part–related superheroes in action.

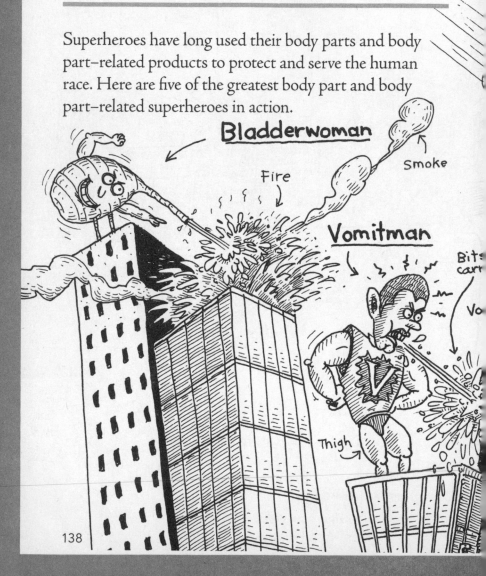

Bladderwoman

Fire

Smoke

Vomitman

Bits carr

Vo

Thigh

SECTION 8

Digestive System

Have you ever wondered what happens to all that cake you shove into your cake hole? Here is everything you need to know about the digestive system.

55. Saliva

Saliva is a fluid that is produced by three salivary glands in your mouth.

When saliva leaves the mouth at high speed, it is called "spit." When saliva leaves the mouth at low speed and dribbles down your chin, it is called "drool" or "slobber."

When saliva froths up and spills out of your mouth in great heaving clumps of foam, it is called "rabies." (If this occurs, see a doctor immediately and try to resist the temptation to bite anyone.)

That is all there is to know about saliva, spit, slobber, drool, and rabies.

A&T'S FUN BODY PART FACT #55

Most experts believe that humans produce between 0.75 and 1.5 quarts of saliva a day, which means that during your lifetime, you'll produce enough to fill one or two swimming pools, though why anybody would want to swim in a swimming pool full of saliva is beyond me.

I've been collecting all my saliva.

56. Esophagus

Your esophagus is the tube that food travels through in order to get to your stomach.

Other easier-to-pronouce names for the esophagus are food funnel, nutrient hose, provisions pipe, chow spout, hamburger highway, taco tunnel, and sausage chute.

That is all there is to know about esophaguses.

A&T'S FUN BODY PART FACT #56

It takes seven seconds for food to travel from the mouth through the esophagus to the stomach.

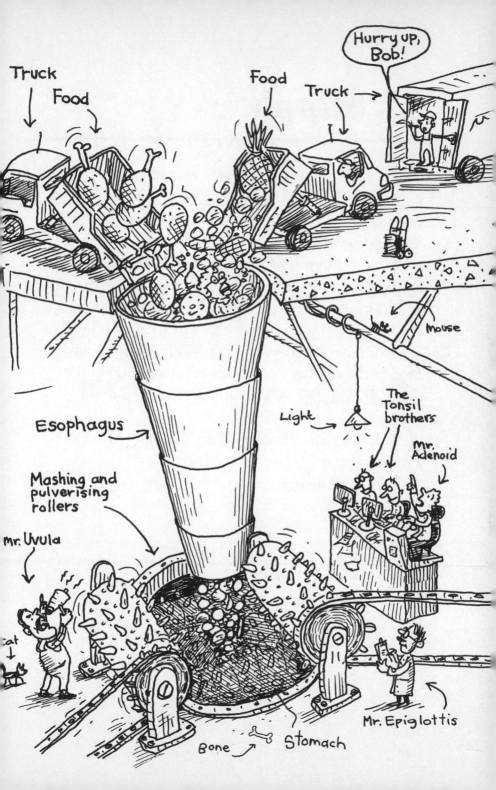

57. Stomach

The stomach is the laziest part of the human body. It treats the other body parts like slaves with its never-ending demands for more food.

This, understandably, leads to great resentment on the part of the eyes, which have to spot the food; the legs, which have to carry the body to the food; the hands, which have to pick the food up, cook it, and put it into the mouth; the teeth, which have to chew the food; the throat, which has to deliver the chewed food to the esophagus, which has to pass it on to the stomach; and the colon, which has to get rid of the waste.

And then, after all that effort, the stomach doesn't even say thanks: It just demands more.

That is all there is to know about stomachs.

A&T'S FUN BODY PART FACT #57

According to scientists, human stomach acid is seriously powerful stuff—so strong, in fact, that it's capable of dissolving razor blades.

58. Small Intestine

There is a widespread belief that if your small intestine was removed from your body and stretched from end to end, it would stretch right around the world.

But I can tell you from personal experience that it actually only stretches about 23 feet and, as we all know, the diameter of the Earth is 7,926 miles.

But if you and 1,820,286 friends all took your intestines out and tied their ends together, I reckon you could definitely do it.

Be warned, though, it's easy enough to get your intestines out, but it's very hard to get them all back in again.

That is all there is to know about small intestines.

Missing piece of Lego

Grrrr!

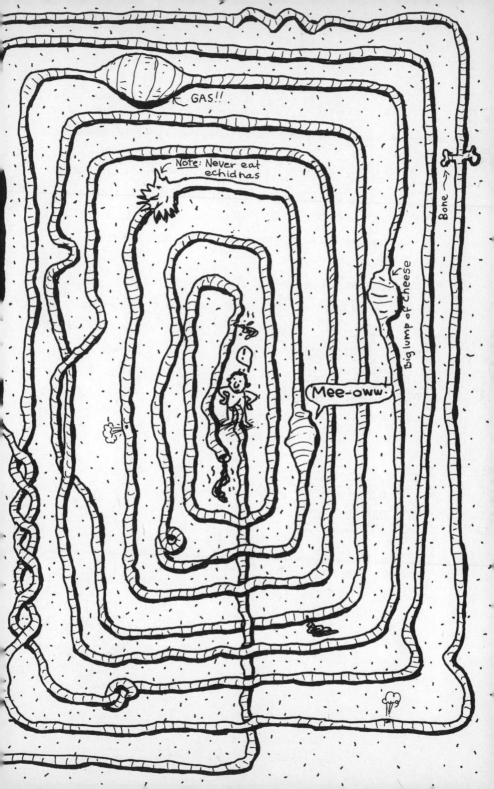

59. Large Intestine

The large intestine is actually much smaller than the small intestine, which is actually much larger than the large intestine, which, as I mentioned, is quite small when compared with the small intestine, which is actually quite large.

Some have suggested that the large intestine should be renamed the not-so-large-in-fact-quite-small intestine, and the small intestine be renamed the not-so-small-in-fact-quite-large intestine, but so far, the opposition to this name change has grown from quite small to very large, whereas support for the name change—which was never very large—has grown quite small.

That is all there is to know about large intestines.

A&T'S FUN BODY PART FACT #60

In your lifetime, your digestive system may handle about 50 tons of food—that's about ten African elephants' worth!

Elephant →

Boy →

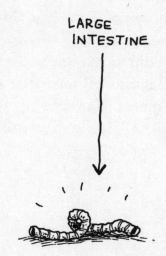

LARGE
INTESTINE

60. Gallbladder

At our school, there used to be a boy called Paul Jones. We used to think it was pretty funny to call him "Gall Stones." That is, until one day in science class, we learned how serious and painful it can be to have gall stones in your gallbladder.

Put simply, gall stones cause some of the worst, most agonizing pain known to man.

After that, it didn't seem quite so clever or funny to call Paul Jones "Gall Stones" anymore, so we called him "Infected Burst Appendix" instead.

That is all there is to know about gallbladders.

A&T'S FUN BODY PART FACT #60

The first gallbladder to reach the summit of Mt. Everest achieved this feat on May 29, 1953. It belonged to the New Zealand mountain climber Sir Edmund Hillary.

61. Liver

The liver is a tough organ. It can take an enormous amount of punishment and still come back for more. To test just how much, I borrowed Terry Denton's liver and smashed it with a sledgehammer about 300 times.

Then I put it in the middle of the road and ran over it with a steamroller.

Then I cut it into strips, dissolved the strips in boiling acid, and then let the acid evaporate until all that was left was just a handful of liver powder.

Then I smashed that with a sledgehammer another 300 times and put what was left back into Terry's body and it's been working fine ever since.

Now that's what I call a tough organ.

That is all there is to know about livers.

A&T'S FUN BODY PART FACT #61

Liver experiments should only be carried out under close medical supervision.

 Two lumps of fat went for a walk one night.

 After a while one fat asked the other, "Do you feel uncomfortable?"

 "I think we are being followed."

 "**Look!** It's a <u>liver</u>!! Run for your life!!"

 The two fats ran like greased lightning... but the <u>liver</u> was faster.

 It trapped the fats down a dead-end alley.

 It looked like the end for the poor little fats.

 SUDDENLY... A <u>pancreas</u> jumped into the alley.

 Caught between a <u>pancreas</u> secreting enzymes...

 ...and an angry liver, the poor little fats had no chance.

 That night, the families of two lumps of fat waited in vain for their loved ones to return.

 Meanwhile the <u>liver</u> and the <u>pancreas</u> celebrated with a late-night kebab.

THE END

TALES OF
THE <u>HUMAN</u> BODY
Number 61: THE LIVER

62. Pancreas

Unlike the liver, the pancreas is *not* a tough organ. Eating too much junk food and not getting enough exercise causes it to shut down. This is called "pancreatic burnout."

This should not be confused with the sort of burnouts you do in a car, which involve squealing tires, lots of smoke, and burning rubber.

Pancreatic burnout is much less exciting: It leads to Type 2 diabetes and lots of other boring health problems, which are much too boring to go into here.

That is all there is to know about pancreases.

A&T'S FUN BODY PART FACT #62

If stomach acid wasn't neutralized by the enzyme made by the pancreas, then your stomach acid would eat through your stomach and digest you alive, from the inside out!

63. Kidneys

If it wasn't for kidneys, we wouldn't have kidney machines, kidney-shaped swimming pools, kidney beans, kidding around, kids' movies, kids' parties, kids' playgrounds, steak and kidney pie, baby goats, or Nicole Kidneyman.

That is all there is to know about kidneys.

A&T'S FUN BODY PART FACT #63

The average person goes to the toilet six times a day.

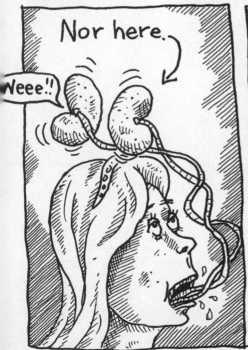

64. Bladder

Drink a glass of water.

Now drink another glass of water.

And another.

And another.

And another.

By now, you should be feeling a familiar pressure in a certain part of your body.

That certain part of your body is called the bladder and that familiar pressure should not be ignored!

That is all there is to know about bladders.

A&T'S FUN BODY PART FACT #64

A full bladder is roughly the size of a softball. But I would not recommend hitting one with a softball bat (especially if you are not wearing a raincoat).

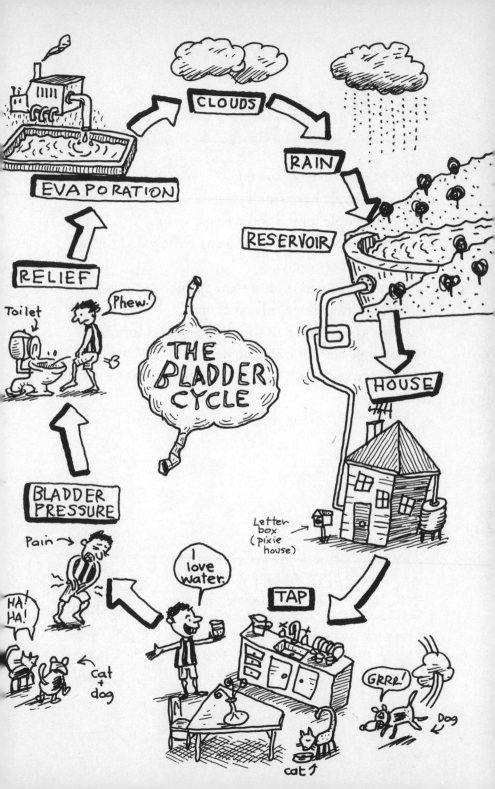

65. Spleen

Some people have big spleens.

Some people have small spleens.

Some people have in-between spleens.

Some people have their spleens removed. This is called a "spleenectomy."

Some people don't have their spleens removed. This is called "not having a spleenectomy."

Some people book in to have a spleenectomy and then change their minds and decide not to have a spleenectomy. This is called "wasting the spleen doctor's time."

That is all there is to know about spleens.

A&T'S FUN BODY PART FACT #65

The spleen was the inspiration for Terry Denton's beloved superhero, Spleenboy. *See* BODY PART AND BODY PART-RELATED SUPERHEROES, page 138.

66. Appendix

Appendixes are the most explosive and action-packed of all the body's organs.

They're always bursting and blowing apart when you least expect it.

And, to make matters worse, nobody even knows why we have the stupid things.

Sure, they leave a cool scar after the doctor has cleaned up the mess and sewn up the hole, but if you want a cool scar, it's much easier—and far less painful— to just draw one on yourself with a marker (*see* SCARS, page 44).

That is all there is to know about appendixes.

A&T'S FUN BODY PART FACT #66

Beware: There is an appendix at the end of this book.

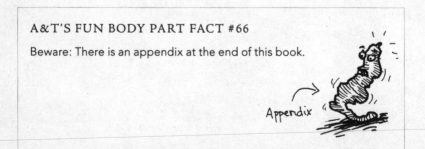

Appendix

67. Private Parts

Private parts are private.

That is not all there is to know about private parts but that is all I can tell you because they are private.

68. Farts

It has long been debated whether farts are a "part" of the human body or merely an unpleasant exhaust product. But what is not debatable is that they are highly flammable.

They are also not as funny as everybody seems to think they are—a fact that you will quickly discover if you are trapped in a room with one.

If you do find yourself trapped in a room with one, open all the windows before trying to find out who was responsible. It's probably best to avoid reporting it to the police, in case the culprit turns out to be you.

That is all there is to know about farts.

A&T'S FUN BODY PART FACT #68

Next time somebody asks you what you want to be when you grow up, tell them you want to be a flatuist (*see* page 71). They probably won't be bothering you again with that silly question for a while.

WHERE DO BODIES COME FROM?

Where do bodies come from? There are many interesting theories, but the truth is that we just don't know.

Delivered by a stork?

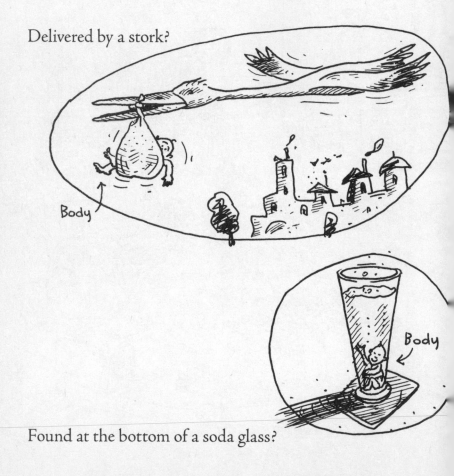

Found at the bottom of a soda glass?

Shot out of a gumball machine?

Hatched from an egg?

Created in a laboratory by a mad scientist?

Appendix 1:
The most disgustingest parts of your body

Peaknuckle: Located just behind the wickenstimmer, the peaknuckle produces mortonium, one of the most lethal and feared of all body products.

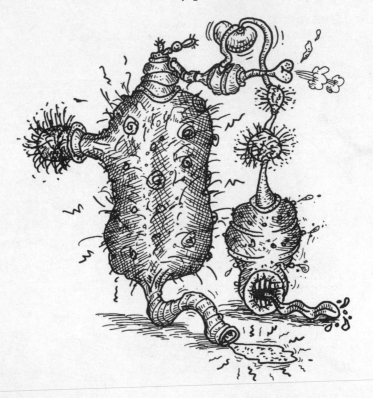

Gingleflop: Emits noxious odors when inflamed. If it goes untreated, you may need to have your body surgically removed.

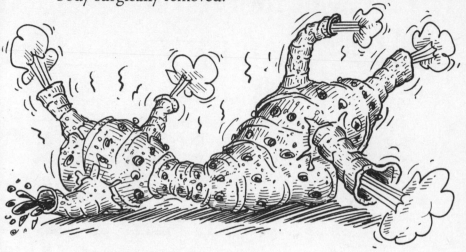

Finknozzle: The less said about the finknozzle the better.

Appendix 2:
The even more disgustingest parts of your body

> **NOTE:** The publisher regrets that this appendix became infected and burst and had to be removed. We apologize for any disappointment or inconvenience this may cause.

COOL-O-METER

Index

W

walking, how to 102–3
Wally 100
Walter's watermelon 30–1
wee-wee 16
wild dogs, protection from
  36–7

windpipe 134
wolf, big bad 26
world, scariest thing
  in the 62

X

xylophone droppings 16